THE GOLDEN BULL

P9-DWE-698

THE GOLDEN BULL

MARJORIE COWLEY

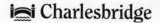 Charlesbridge

Of enormous help to me in writing this book were family and friends, the counsel of my writers' group, and eminent scholars in the vast field of ancient Mesopotamia who answered my endless questions with endless patience. My deepest appreciation to you all.—M. C.

First paperback edition 2012
Text copyright © 2008 by Marjorie Cowley
All rights reserved, including the right of reproduction in whole or in part in any form.
Charlesbridge and colophon are registered trademarks of Charlesbridge Publishing, Inc.

Published by Charlesbridge
85 Main Street
Watertown, MA 02472
(617) 926-0329
www.charlesbridge.com

Library of Congress Cataloging-in-Publication Data
Cowley, Marjorie.
    The golden bull / Marjorie Cowley.
        p. cm.
    Summary: During a severe drought in Mesopotamia in 2600 B.C., when their parents
can no longer support them, Jomar and his sister Zefa are sent to the city of Ur, where
Jomar is apprenticed to a goldsmith and Zefa must try to find a way to keep from
becoming a slave. Includes author's note on the history of the region.
    ISBN 978-1-58089-181-3 (reinforced for library use)
    ISBN 978-1-58089-182-0 (softcover)
    ISBN 978-1-60734-527-5 (ebook)
    ISBN 978-1-60734-253-3 (ebook pdf)
    1. Iraq—History—To 634—Juvenile fiction. [1. Iraq—History—To 634—Fiction.
2. Brothers and sisters—Fiction. 3. Apprentices—Fiction.] I. Title.
PZ7.C8377Go 2008
[Fic]—dc22   2007042620

Printed in the United States of America
(hc) 10 9 8 7 6 5 4 3 2 1
(sc) 10 9 8 7 6 5 4 3

Display type set in Mighty Tuxedo and text type set in Monotype Centaur
Color separations by Chroma Graphics, Singapore
Printed by Worzalla Publishing Company in Stevens Point, Wisconsin, USA
Production supervision by Brian G. Walker
Designed by Susan Mallory Sherman

TABLE OF CONTENTS

LIST OF CHARACTERS

Jomar (JOH-mar): Son of a farmer

Zefa (ZEH-fah): Jomar's younger sister

Durabi (dur-AH-bee): Father

Lilan (LEE-lan): Mother

Malak (MAL-ak): Temple official

Qat-Nu (CAT-noo): Slave

Sidah (SEE-dah): Goldsmith

Nari (NAH-ree): Sidah's wife

Abban (AH-ban): Sidah's son (deceased)

Gamil (GAH-mil): Abban's friend

Bittatti (bih-TAH-tee): High priestess

Kurgal (KUR-gall): Temple music director

1 CHANGES

The drought had lasted for months. Jomar dug for edible roots in the dry, sandy soil, but found only three small, misshapen carrots that once he would have given to the pigs. He glanced up at the squawking blackbirds as they flew high above him. When he was younger, it had been his job to wave his arms and yell at the birds to scare them off before they ate the precious barley seeds. Now they no longer swooped down to pick at the brown and brittle grain.

Jomar stopped digging when he heard the bellowing of a cow. He had promised his father to help with the birthing of her calf.

As he ran across the scorched fields toward the cowshed, the rocky soil cut into his frayed leather sandals. The entire region was so barren that it was hard for Jomar to recall that all the farms in the area had once produced abundant grain, melons and grapes, plums and pears, cabbage and carrots. Gazelle and other wild animals had once been plentiful, attracted to the crops and to the water in the irrigation canals that cut through the countryside. Now the canals were empty, and the farm looked as if nothing had ever grown in the sunbaked land that stretched around him.

Jomar heard his younger sister, Zefa, singing as he passed the goat hutch. As she sang she strummed on a small wooden lyre, a stringed instrument he'd made for her when she was a little girl.

Veering from the path to the cowshed, Jomar darted into the hutch. Zefa sat on an overturned bucket, so intent on her song that she didn't look up at him. Squinting into the shadows, he saw that Zefa's eyes glistened like pieces of glassy black obsidian as she began a song to Nanna, the mighty moongod:

> *"Moon-glowing Nanna,*
> *all-knowing Nanna,*
> *Look down from the heavens*
> *and pity us—"*

Jomar broke in. "Pity! What pity? Why make up a song to the moongod when he lets his people go hungry?" He didn't wait for an answer. "And don't let Father hear this sad song—he's worried enough as it is." He turned to leave the hutch.

"Wait," Zefa said. "I'm in here so he *won't* hear me, but you should listen. This will be the last time you'll hear my music."

He stared at her and realized why her eyes glistened—they were filled with tears. "What do you mean? Why are you crying?"

Zefa gave her news haltingly. "I heard Father talking to Mother last night. They thought I was asleep. Tomorrow he's sending you away . . . to the city . . . to live in Ur."

Jomar's breath went out of him. "I don't believe this! You're sure?"

"There's not enough food for us all," Zefa said. "Haven't you noticed they're growing weaker?"

"Yes, I've noticed," Jomar said, but he knew he had been pushing this knowledge away. Too full of hurt and anger to talk further, and aching to escape from his sister's sad eyes, Jomar abruptly left the hutch. His mouth was dry; he could feel his heart pounding. Where would he live in the city? What would he do there? Farming was all he knew and all he wanted to know.

Trying to calm himself, Jomar looked out across the flat fields and saw the massive mud-brick temple of Ur looming in the distance like a mountain. Nanna, the powerful moongod of Ur, lived in the temple. Jomar had grown up feeling protected by him, but now he felt abandoned by Nanna. And by his father.

Again he heard the bellowing of the cow. Again he'd forgotten his promise to help with the birth of her calf. He started running, but dread as well as hunger made his stomach tighten with cramps. Because of the drought two boys his age who lived in surrounding farms had been sold into slavery in exchange for food. *Would my father do that to me?* It was unthinkable, but he could think of nothing else as he raced toward the cowshed.

2 HARD TIMES

Jomar burst into the shed and found his father, Durabi, kneeling over a newborn calf struggling to free itself from its birth pouch.

"The birthing was hard . . . the little one's so weak," his father said. "It must be released from its pouch so it can nurse." Durabi handed Jomar his knife, sat back on his heels, and stared at his son with dull eyes.

Jomar took the knife and cut open the pouch that imprisoned the calf. He brought the newborn to its feet, stroking the small, slippery creature that had somehow survived its difficult delivery. Then Jomar lifted the calf to its mother, but it was so wobbly that he had to put his arms around its body to keep it from falling. The cow turned to lick her offspring as it nursed.

Jomar saw his father watching him, his face creased with care. Was his father worried about the calf? Their last cow, so thin that her ribs could be counted? Or was he worried about him?

Jomar raised his chin and blurted out his concern. "Zefa said you're sending me away to the city. This can't be true!"

His father winced, but the silence in the hot shed was broken only by the noise of the newborn calf's weak suckling.

"Father, speak to me!" Jomar persisted. "I'm needed here."

"The farm grows nothing," Durabi said bitterly. "Our barley is gone, and the only wheat left is emmer." He picked up some of the hard, reddish grain on the floor and let it slip through his fingers. "We planted this to feed our animals. Now it feeds us."

"Yes, I know, but—"

Durabi continued as if he hadn't heard. "Our pigs and sheep are gone . . . taken by the temple, traded for barley, or slaughtered to keep us alive." He pointed to Jomar's worn sandals and shook his head. "Without hide I can't even make you a new pair."

"Father, listen! I know nothing but farming. What will I do in the city?"

"I haven't told you this because I prayed that the snows would melt . . . ." He faltered, then gathered his strength. "The last time I was in Ur—to give my last two pigs to the temple—I stopped at a bazaar to eat my midday meal. There I met a man named Sidah, a goldsmith who works for the temple. We talked. I told him I feared I would have to send you to the city to survive because of desperate conditions on the farm. He told me his only child, a son about your age, had recently died. Sidah and I made an agreement. . . ." Again he stopped speaking, and looked away. "You will be his new apprentice."

"I have no interest in being a goldsmith's apprentice!" Jomar's throat closed up and his words came out in a whisper. "Will I be his slave?"

"He'll take you into his house and teach you his skills, but I didn't sell you to him," Durabi said. "How could I do this to you? Or to your sister?"

Jomar stared at his father. "Zefa?"

"She must go with you," Durabi said. "She grows too thin, and her hair has lost its luster."

"This isn't fair! How can I learn new skills and look after her at the same time?"

"You can't," Durabi answered. "She must have her own work."

"And what would that be?" Jomar asked in a challenging tone he had never used with his father before.

Durabi bit off his words. "I made no arrangements for her because I had no thought of sending her away. You're fourteen—soon you'll be a man. Zefa will be your responsibility."

Jomar felt his stomach hollow out. "I beg you, Father, let us both stay. The snows will melt, the river will run full again, and the canals and reservoirs will fill with water. Then you'll need me to help with the replanting. Mother will need Zefa to help with her chores."

Durabi shook his head sadly, the anger drained out of him. "I can't wait any longer—I must act before you and Zefa weaken. The arrangement I've made for you with the goldsmith is good. Early tomorrow morning I'll take you to the broad, well-traveled road that leads to the city. You must stay on it until you get to the great gate of Ur."

"You're not taking us all the way?" Jomar asked, embarrassed by the catch in his voice.

"That was my first thought, but your mother's too weak for me to leave her for that long a time," Durabi said. "She's been giving you and Zefa most of her food, pretending that she's eaten earlier or will eat later."

Jomar's anger lifted as he listened to his father's words and saw his sorrowful expression. "When did you make your decision to send Zefa to the city?" he asked softly.

"Only yesterday afternoon, when I found our last two goats dead of starvation in the far field," Durabi said. "They were nothing but bones, their hair matted and coarse. I thought of Zefa's hair . . . how it used to shine. . . ." He let the words fade away.

The calf stopped nursing and made small, plaintive noises. There was no more milk. The cow bent her scrawny neck to lick her newborn again. Jomar felt his future was as shaky as the calf's. He was certain of only one thing: he would not be here to find out if this small, struggling creature lived or died.

3 PREPARATIONS

Jomar turned restlessly on his narrow cot throughout the hot night. He felt the gritty sting of sand that had drifted into the house in spite of his mother's unending efforts to sweep it out. How completely his life would change when the darkness lightened into dawn. Not only was he being forced to leave, but in the city he would have the heavy burden of caring for Zefa.

Jomar must have finally dozed, because the familiar scent of sesame woke him. His mother came in carrying a lamp that burned the pungent oil made from crushed sesame seeds.

"My son, my son," Lilan crooned, putting down the lamp and kneeling beside his bed. "I never wanted this to happen to you, to Zefa," she said, burying her face in her hands.

"I know you didn't," Jomar said, taking her hands

away from her thin, lined face and holding them in his own. "Has Zefa found out what's going to happen to her?"

"I took her up to the roof last evening to tell her," Lilan said. "She cried in my arms like a toddling child through half the night. Oh, Jomar, help her. Her strong spirit has fled."

"I don't think she'll let me help her—she's always gone to you when she's needed comforting." Jomar stopped talking as Zefa came down the ladder from the roof. Rumpled and red-eyed, she stared sullenly at Jomar as if this upheaval were his fault.

Lilan stood up and brushed the tears from her eyes. "The journey to the city will take a full day. You must leave soon so you'll have some cool walking time before sunrise." She brought out two reed traveling baskets. "Both of you have a change of clothing and what food I could give you. You must make it last until you get to Ur."

Durabi appeared in the low doorway. "I've come from the cowshed. The little one is weak and needs more milk than its mother can give it, but it survived the night."

"Good news, Father," Jomar said, then busied himself attaching his basket to his back and adjusting its leather straps.

Zefa rummaged in her basket. "My lyre isn't here!"

Lilan patted her arm. "I didn't want to burden you with anything unnecessary."

"Your basket's heavy enough," Jomar said, thinking that he would have to shoulder it along with his own when Zefa got tired.

But Zefa spoke slowly, emphasizing each word. "I want my lyre."

Lilan stroked her daughter's face, then added the instrument to Zefa's belongings. When she hung the basket from Zefa's thin shoulders, her mother received the glimmering of a smile. Jomar received an angry look.

Durabi turned to Jomar. "I've heard a guard has been stationed at the city gate during these troubled times. When he asks your reason for entering the city, tell them you are to be apprenticed to Sidah, a temple goldsmith."

"You're working for a goldsmith?" Zefa asked, wide-eyed. "What will I do?"

"Work will be found for you," Durabi said quickly, then turned to Jomar. "Sidah told me that his house is on a street in the back of the temple where craftsmen live. When you find him, present yourself as the son of Durabi."

"And Zefa?" Jomar asked.

"I've told you what your responsibilities are," his father said.

When Jomar frowned, Zefa glared at him with narrowed eyes.

"Go while it's still cool," Lilan said. Now openly weeping, she drew her children to her and touched each of their faces tenderly. "We do this for you . . . only for you."

Durabi patted his wife's shoulder. "I'll return as soon as I can."

Jomar, Zefa, and their father went out through the low doorway into the still-dark morning. They could hear Lilan's soft, insistent crying as they walked away from the farmhouse. Finally the only sound heard was the slap-slap of their sandals on the hard, dry ground.

4 ON THEIR WAY

Too numbed to talk, they walked along the sandy road in silence. The sky grew brighter, then the edge of the sun appeared on the flat horizon. Gradually the cool of the night disappeared as the blazing circle rose slowly in the sky. The heat increased until it became so intense that Jomar thought he could see rays of sunlight shimmering in front of him.

Jomar walked beside his father, who was holding Zefa's hand. Without warning, Durabi swayed, then pitched forward. In an instant Zefa was down beside him, cradling her father's head in her lap.

Jomar knelt down and spoke quietly. "Father, you're too weak to make this journey. I know you wanted to be sure we took the right road, but I can find it from your description. Stay here until you feel stronger, then go back to the farm."

Durabi raised himself to a sitting position and

started to protest, then sank down again. "I wanted to take you to the city, and now I'm unable to take you to the road that leads to the city. Go on without me—you must be in Ur before nightfall."

They helped their father settle under an almost-leafless tree that offered a bit of shade. Durabi pressed Zefa to his chest, his hands smoothing her hair. He looked at Jomar with teary eyes. "You must have better sandals. Mine are newer. Take them and give me yours." After the exchange was made, he reached up and embraced Jomar. "I know Zefa will be in good hands."

Aware their father was watching them, Jomar and Zefa started off at a rapid pace. But when the road curved and they knew Durabi could no longer see them, Zefa's steps began to falter. She fell farther and farther behind.

Jomar stopped. "Try to go faster," he called back to her. "I'll wait for you."

"Not fair!" Zefa shouted back. "While you wait, you'll be resting."

"If you keep up with me, we can rest together," Jomar yelled.

"I'm hungry, and tired of walking," Zefa said as she reached him.

Jomar sighed and pointed to some yellowing tamarisk trees growing close to a reservoir some distance ahead. "Maybe there's a swallow of drinking water there. Anyway, we need to get out of the sun for a while."

But the reservoir held just a rubble of rocks, silty dried mud, and a trickle of stagnant water. Kicking off their sandals, they sank to the ground under the meager shade of the trees.

Jomar opened his basket. Only a small clay bowl, a handful of dates, and four small, shrunken pomegranates.

Zefa wrinkled her nose. "They look like dried-up pieces of leather."

Jomar said nothing. Removing the top of the bowl, he found a thick porridge made of boiled emmer, the wheat they grew to feed their animals. "This'll fill us up."

"But it's tasteless," Zefa said.

"That's all I have," Jomar said sharply. "What's in yours?"

Zefa took a woven pouch from her basket and untied its reed string. She showed Jomar a small mixture of almonds and hard raisins. Searching deeper, she found a boiled egg still in its shell and held it up as if it were a carved ivory treasure. "Mother gave me the last one," she said tearily.

Their mother was right: Zefa's spirit was gone indeed. Mothers knew how to help, but what could a brother do to make his sister strong?

Jomar could only think of one thing. "Eat."

She looked lovingly at the egg, then stuffed more than half of it into her mouth.

"Share the food!" Jomar said.

Zefa began weeping. "You told me to eat."

"All right, I did," Jomar said. "We'll divide the egg and dates between us and save the rest for the long walk ahead of us."

Zefa raised her chin. "Why are you the one who makes all the decisions?"

"I'm in charge because I'm older than you," Jomar answered.

Zefa shook her head angrily. "You've gone from ignoring me to ordering me around."

"It's a job I don't want!"

"Don't try to make me feel sorry for you." Zefa's tone changed. "I'll give you what's left of the egg for one of your dates."

Exasperated, he handed her a shriveled date.

"I wish it was a syrupy one that Mother saved to make into honey."

"You know they were gone a long time ago." Jomar looked at Zefa, thin and miserable. His eye fell on her basket. The lyre was inside. "Sing a song for me." He felt his cheeks flush. "The one you were singing in the goat hutch when I made you stop."

Zefa's eyes widened with surprise. She swallowed the date, her face brightening as she brought out her lyre. She began to sing with her head tilted back, her eyes closed.

"Moon-glowing Nanna,
all-knowing Nanna,
Look down from the heavens
and pity us, born only to serve you;
Comfort us, born only to serve you.

Moon-glowing Nanna,
all-knowing Nanna,
Look down from the heavens
and pity us,
comfort us, weep for us.
Your tears will water our wasted land."

Jomar chewed his bit of egg slowly as he listened to her soaring voice. For years he'd heard the songs that Zefa made up, heard them without really listening. They had been about such childish things as a lost doll, the death of a pig, and the sun's magic that shriveled a grape into a sweet raisin. But now Jomar was struck by the words of this song. How could a girl of twelve make up such a solemn prayer?

As Zefa was repeating the last line of her song, rustling sounds behind him made Jomar wheel around. A dozen men stood gazing at Zefa with rapt expressions. He had no idea how long they'd been there.

5 "A GOOD VOICE"

Jomar sprang to his feet and stood over Zefa, his hand gripping her shoulder. Zefa stopped singing, opened her eyes, and saw the group gathered in front of them. She looked up at Jomar with alarm.

A tall, heavyset man stepped forward. His fine linen garment stretched tight across his large belly. The men behind him wore frayed sandals and rough cotton tunics that hung loosely on their thin frames. All carried knives attached to their belts, and digging tools rested on their shoulders.

Gesturing toward Zefa, the stout man spoke to Jomar. "A good voice, a good musician—surprising for one so young."

Jomar tried not to show his fear or anger. Hadn't he urged Zefa to leave her lyre behind? This man who spoke with such easy authority could only cause trouble.

"Why are you two on the road alone?" The man emphasized the last word of his question.

"I go to Ur to be an apprentice to Sidah, a temple goldsmith," Jomar said.

The man studied Zefa with calculating eyes. "And the little lyre player? What will she do?"

"I'll find work for her," Jomar said.

The man shook his head. "That'll be hard to do in the city, but there's work to be done here. I'm Malak, sent by the temple to patrol the irrigation system and see that it's clear of rubble." He glared at the men. "The moongod is displeased with you farmers for letting the canals and reservoirs fill with rocks, dead plants, and silt. You've forgotten that you live and work on land that is owned by Nanna's temple."

The sullen men were silent until one spoke out. "We've kept the waterways clear in the past, but the long drought has made us lose hope."

Malak turned to Jomar. "These farmers have no faith that the moongod will eventually provide for his people. Soon you'll be a man, so you must join my crew."

"I can't. The goldsmith waits for me," Jomar said. "But when the drought is over and I return to our farm, I'll gladly join your work crew."

Malak snorted. "When you return? It's the custom that an apprentice can leave only if he's been poorly taught."

Jomar was stunned. Raised in the country, he knew nothing of city rules that governed craftsmen and their apprentices.

Malak dipped his head in mock courtesy. "Be on your way to this man who works with glorious gold. The girl will stay to help with meals and keep up the spirits of the men with her music."

"You can't separate us." Jomar's hand tightened on Zefa's shoulder. "She's my sister."

"Ah, but I can," Malak said. "I'm a temple official with the authority to enslave any child found wandering far from home without a parent."

"But she has parents!" Jomar cried out.

Malak slowly looked around. "I do not see them." He turned to Zefa. "You're thin. You'll be well fed in return for your work."

Jomar felt weak. With an effort he pulled his

eyes away from Malak and looked at the other men. Most seemed sympathetic, but a few looked more entertained than concerned. Two men with their heads thrust forward toward Zefa frightened him.

"I'll join your work force," Jomar said quietly. He felt Zefa's shoulder sag with relief under his grip.

A thin smile played on Malak's lips. "You will receive Nanna's blessing for your efforts." The smirk disappeared. "I've wasted enough time with the two of you. Girl, see that old man stirring the pot? Help him prepare the evening meal."

Jomar bent down to whisper a promise of protection to Zefa, words he knew would be difficult for him to uphold.

Malak's hand cut the air. "Leave her! There's work to be done."

6 TRAPPED

Malak took the lead, heading off with short, fast steps. But under the scorching sun, his pace soon slowed and his bald head gleamed with sweat. The silent men walked behind Malak in a haze of dust and dirt scuffed up by their feet. Jomar, near the end of the line, had grit in his eyes, his mouth, his nose.

"We were next to a reservoir that needed work," Jomar said quietly to the man nearest to him. "Why are we leaving?"

The man looked straight ahead. "First we must clear a canal some distance away." He pointed his chin at Malak. "When we're close to exhaustion, he'll have us return to clean out the reservoir before he lets us eat or sleep."

"He's cruel," Jomar said.

The man shrugged. "Cruel and clever. He knows how to get work out of the farmers. If their labor pleases him, they'll have a good meal and all the beer they can drink tonight."

"You sound like you've done this kind of thing before," Jomar said.

"Many times for many years," the man said. "I'm Qat-nu, a temple slave assigned to travel the farm-lands with Malak." He turned slightly so that his bare back, covered with welts and jagged scars, could be seen by Jomar. "Marks of his displeasure."

Horrified, Jomar stared at Qat-nu's back.

Qat-nu looked at Jomar with a sorrowful expression on his wrinkled, sunburned face. "I pity your young sister. Both of you must do your work well and give Malak no cause for anger. I'll leave your side because it will go poorly with me if he sees me talking to you." Qat-nu lost himself among the other men.

The crew came to a halt at the bank of a debris-filled canal that had once carried water to neighboring fields. "Remove the loose rocks from the canal and put them on the banks," Malak ordered. "Shovel out the silt and spread it on the ground. Rebuild the collapsed banks with the rocks to hold the water that will someday return." He settled under a yellowing palm tree, the only shady spot in the parched field. Soon his eyes were half-closed.

The work called for no special skill, only endurance. Without a shovel to remove the caked mud, Jomar collected and stacked the rocks that the others heaved out of the canal.

The hot, dusty day wore on. The ache in Jomar's back gradually increased and his hands became covered with cuts from the sharp, jagged rocks he handled. He listened to a steady, soft rumble of complaints from the men who worked close to him.

"What right do they have to take us from our farms? Let slaves do this work."

"I treat my animals better than he treats us."

"My mouth feels like a desert—I need something to drink!"

Only Qat-nu was silent. Jomar guessed that a slave had no right to complain. To avoid Malak's anger Jomar stayed as silent as the slave.

After the canal had been cleared, Qat-nu woke Malak, who had been sleeping with his head lolling to one side. Malak rubbed his eyes and lurched to his feet.

"Your tasks here are finished," Malak barked while tugging at a small silver flask that hung from his belt. "We return now to clear the reservoir." When he put the flask to his lips and drank, there was angry muttering. "See that the work is finished before the sun disappears," he said. "Tomorrow you'll repair the other canals that you farmers have ignored."

Tomorrow. They had expected to be in the city tonight. They were trapped, unable to escape Malak's powerful hold on them both.

7 GODDESS OF BEER

In the late afternoon Jomar and the crew left the canal and walked through the camp to reach the reservoir. Zefa, stirring food in a large, blackened bowl, raised her hand in greeting when she saw Jomar.

"Girl, pay attention to your work," came Malak's low growl.

Zefa returned to stirring the pot that rested on dull embers. When Jomar breathed in the smells of lamb and onion stew, he knew Qat-nu had spoken the truth: the men would be rewarded with abundant food.

As the crew left the camp, Malak settled down in the shade next to another large pot. This one sat on a three-legged stand and had a ladle attached to it with braided flax.

Without a word being exchanged between Malak and the slave, Qat-nu led Jomar and the others to a reservoir a short distance away. Once there Qat-nu gave directions in a clear, calm voice as he worked alongside the men. There were fewer muttered complaints. In spite of hunger and fatigue, the men briskly cleared the reservoir of debris.

They returned to camp at dusk to line up for food. Zefa and the old man scooped out the stew with chunks of freshly baked flat bread and distributed the meal to those in line. She did not look up at Jomar when he stood in front of her.

It was the largest portion of food that Jomar had seen in a long time, and he crammed the delicious meal into his mouth. He could tell by the taste and light color of the bread that it had been made from wheat, not the coarse and flavorless emmer that his family had been forced to eat. Jomar sought out Qat-nu. "Where did this wheat come from?"

"The temple granaries have great stores of food gathered from all the farmlands," Qat-nu answered.

"Our crops have failed." Jomar's voice rose. "Our own storage bins are empty. We go hungry!"

Qat-nu hushed him with a finger to his lips. "The farmers do without so that the city of Ur may flourish. The temple takes a portion of food and animals from the farms to feed its officials, workers, and craftsmen," he said quietly.

The farmers stopped eating when they saw Zefa and the old man struggle to move the large pot with the attached ladle to the center of the cooking area.

Malak, on his feet and swaying, gestured for the men to come and drink. They surged around the brew pot, swilling down gulps of beer and spitting out the barley husks that floated on the surface. Although his throat was scratchy from the dust, Jomar took only one swallow. He must stay alert for whatever lay ahead.

Malak pointed to Zefa, who was finishing her meal. "Sing for us, girl!" Although his speech was slurred, his tone was one of command.

With a startled look Zefa glanced at her brother. Jomar nodded.

"Shall I sing again about the moongod Nanna, or a song to the sungod Utu?" she asked in a shaky voice.

Malak snorted. "Neither! Sing to Ninkasi, the goddess of beer."

Zefa's voice shook. "I have no song to her."

"Make one up!" Malak ordered.

Zefa pulled out her lyre. She sat on the ground with her head down and strummed on the instrument for a long, awkward time.

An angry voice rang out. "Begin!"

"Play!" said another.

Jomar wanted to shout at her, too. Instead he tried to imitate the calm, clear voice that Qat-nu had used at the reservoir. "She'll sing when she's ready."

Zefa took a deep breath and began her song hesitantly, almost in a whisper. Slowly her voice gathered force and the song took on a lilting beat:

> *"Hail to Ninkasi who fills the mouth with beer,*
> *Brown barley beer.*
> *Hail to Ninkasi who taught us to make the beer,*
> *Brown barley beer.*
> *Hail to Ninkasi who knew honey froths the beer,*
> *Brown barley beer.*
> *Hail to Ninkasi who fills the mouth with beer,*
> *Brown barley beer."*

The men listened avidly, and Jomar let out his breath with relief. Where had she learned to make up such a rollicking drinking song?

The men shouted to Zefa to sing the song again, and Jomar saw that her face was flushed with pleasure at her success. Milling around the brew pot, the men clapped their hands and joined lustily in the singing. "Again, again," they shouted, but when they pushed in around her, Zefa paled and her words faltered. She held her lyre against her chest like a shield.

Alarmed, Jomar looked to the slave for guidance.

"A wrestling match!" Qat-nu shouted above the din. He looked at Jomar and pointed toward Malak who lay sprawled in a stupor on a sheepskin robe with his mouth open, his eyes closed.

Jomar snatched up Zefa's basket. Shoving his way through the crowd, he pulled her from the center of the group. There were angry howls of protest. Some of the men tried to stop them from leaving by grabbing at their arms, their clothes. Zefa clutched her lyre with both hands.

"Who will come forward to fight?" Qat-nu yelled. "The winner will take home a sack of lentils!"

The boisterous farmers turned their attention to the match, circling around the two men who had volunteered to wrestle. An area was cleared for the contest. Bets were placed as the name of one fighter, then the other, was shouted out.

Jomar tugged at Zefa's arm, then motioned for her to follow him. Glancing back he saw the wrestlers rubbing oil on their bodies.

"Now, Zefa, now!" Jomar said, breaking into a run. "This is our chance!"

8 THE MOONLIT ROAD

With only a slender new moon to see by, Jomar was unsure which road they were on. He ran hard, his only thought to get away from the camp. Fear made them both light-footed and fleet.

Jomar heard thrashing sounds nearby.

"We're after you!" came a slurred voice out of the shadows. "The slave girl will pay for this—and so will you!" It was Malak, and he was not alone.

There were more confused, crashing noises as the drunken men tried to hunt them down. Then a heavy thud. Malak spoke no more, but others did.

"Now we'll have to lug him back to camp—"

"It'll take the three of us to do it."

"We'll miss the fight!"

"Glad they escaped—wish I were with 'em."

More muffled commotion. They heard a faint dragging sound. Then silence.

Jomar made out a different road ahead and took it, running until his breath gave out. Unable to stop in time, Zefa ran into him. They hung on to each other until their heavy, painful breathing returned to an even rhythm.

Jomar searched the area for the road to Ur, but paths were everywhere. He dropped to his knees, running his hands across the dust and dirt to discover by touch what he could not see. Finally Jomar stood up. "This is the road to the city. It's wide and heavily grooved by cart wheels."

As they walked they heard the faint, faraway shouts of men watching the wrestling match. Soon the night swallowed all sounds except the buzz of insects and the steady slap-slap of their sandals on the moonlit road.

Jomar broke the silence. "Your lyre got us into trouble again."

Zefa stood still. "You're blaming me? You nodded when Malak ordered me to sing."

"Keep walking. I was frightened at what he might do if you refused, but you certainly looked happy when the men begged you to sing over and over again."

"What's wrong with being happy when people like my music?" Zefa said. "My favorite pig was more interested in my songs than you ever were!"

Jomar tried to cut her off. "At least we're safe and on our way to Ur."

"Safe! You'll be safe, but Malak"—Zefa spat out his name—"has made me a slave!"

Worse than a slave—a runaway slave, Jomar said to himself. "Ur is so big that no one will know what Malak has done." Jomar hoped this might be so. "And I'll find some work for you to do." Another easy promise.

Zefa shook her head. "In the city, no one will need me to care for newborn pigs or spin sheep's wool into yarn."

Again Jomar changed the subject. "Your song, Zefa. How did you come to know the rhythm of a drinking song?"

"Last year I heard farmers and herdsmen singing when they gathered near our house to drink beer and sleep in the fields," Zefa said. "Father went with them to the city the next morning to bring the grain and livestock that the temple demanded."

Jomar kicked at a few stray dirt clods. "Our barley could have made the very beer that Malak was guzzling."

"It doesn't matter where the barley came from," Zefa said. "We couldn't have escaped if he hadn't gotten drunk."

Jomar sighed. "But it was the slave who thought of the wrestling match so we could get away."

Zefa's voice grew soft. "I hope someday the gods will reward him for his kindness to us."

Jomar thought about the fresh wounds that would appear on the slave's back if Malak suspected he had helped them escape. "Yes, Qat-nu was kind and brave."

The cool of the night helped them walk at a fast pace. They shared Zefa's almonds and raisins between them, eating slowly to make them last longer.

Zefa stopped again and shivered. "Everything looks so strange . . . scary."

Jomar gazed around him. The land, white with evaporated salt caused by the drought, was bathed by eerie moonlight that made it look even whiter. "It does look strange, but we have to keep walking."

They trudged on until Zefa held up her hand. "Listen! A baby's crying."

Around a bend, three men and two women sat huddled for warmth around a small fire by the side of the road. One woman held a wriggling, wailing baby in her arms.

"They can't quiet that baby," Jomar whispered. "Don't stop."

Zefa ignored him and walked toward the people crouched around the low flames.

Jomar caught up with her and pulled at her sleeve. "We've had enough trouble for one day. I don't want to spend much time here."

Straining to be heard over the baby's cries, Jomar spoke to the oldest man. "My sister and I need food to complete our journey to the city. Do you have some you can spare?"

"We were turned back at the gate, so we must save what's left of our food for the journey home," the man answered. "Be warned—unless you can show that you have business or employment in Ur, you'll be denied entrance."

Jomar glanced nervously at Zefa. How would he

get her into the city? He pointed behind him. "We've just escaped from a work crew. You must stay away from a temple official called Malak who will force you to help clear the waterways."

The man nodded his thanks. The mother stood, holding her baby over her shoulder. She paced in a wide circle around the fire, yet still the baby wailed.

"My boy cries for milk, but his mother has little to give him," the man said. "We have only one she-goat left on our farm. When we get home, I hope her milk can nourish my son."

Zefa took out her lyre and began strumming a shower of notes, then leaned close to the baby:

> *"Don't weep,*
> *Black-eyed baby boy,*
> *Don't weep.*
> *Sleep soft,*
> *Black-eyed baby boy,*
> *Sleep deep."*

She sang the lullaby first in a strong voice, then softly, and finally the words disappeared into a soothing hum. The baby's wails were now inter-spersed by silence, as if he listened between sobs. Suddenly he stopped crying, put his head in the crook of his mother's neck, and fell asleep. Zefa's rhythmic strumming continued for a few more mo-ments, then her hands were still.

"Thank the gods, he's sleeping," the mother whispered.

The baby's father looked at Zefa. "It's you we thank, girl." He spread a small square of cloth on the ground. Quickly and quietly each person brought out a small amount of food and placed it on the cloth. The father tied the corners together and thrust it into Jomar's hands. "This exchange was fair and good," he said. "You will see the gates of the city before noon to-morrow. May you find what you seek in Ur."

9 GREAT GATE OF UR

Jomar took the food and bowed his head in gratitude, then he and Zefa left the group. When they turned to wave farewell, they saw sheepskins already unrolled and spread out on the ground in preparation for their long-delayed rest.

Jomar patted Zefa on her back. "Singing to that baby was a good way to get food."

"That isn't why I did it," Zefa said, "but I noticed they gave the food to you, not me."

"It's because I'm the oldest," Jomar said.

Zefa shook her head. "Unfair." She slipped the reed basket off her back. "They're sleeping—what about us?"

"Mother thought we'd be in Ur by nightfall, so we have no blankets," Jomar said.

"I'm too tired to need bedding." Without another

word, Zefa shook out her loose braids, then stretched out on the ground by the side of the road.

Jomar lay down beside her, cradling his head in his arms. He hummed Zefa's lullaby and sank into an exhausted sleep like the baby on his mother's shoulder.

When he awoke, the warmth of the new day covered him like a thin cotton blanket. He looked at Zefa, still sleeping. The strain on her face had been smoothed away by rest. "Wake up, Zefa. The sungod begins his ride across the sky."

Zefa gave a small moan and sat up. She ran her hands through her hair and began braiding it. Father was right: her long, black hair no longer shone. He touched her shoulder gently. "Your song helped me get to sleep."

Zefa smiled. "It was almost the same lullaby I sang to my favorite pig after it was born. Instead of 'black-eyed baby boy,' I used to sing 'pink-eyed pretty pig.'"

He smiled back at her, then realized this was the first time on their journey that he had done so.

They started out again, but now they were not alone on the rutted road. Where had these people been last night? Had they, too, slept by the side of

the road or bedded down in empty fields? Most of
the travelers going toward the city were rawboned
single men carrying heavy burdens on their shoulders. Looking slightly more prosperous, a few men
walked beside loaded wooden carts pulled by small,
straining donkeys. The families with dawdling young
children traveled slowly. The people moving in the
opposite direction looked defeated, their shoulders
hunched and their eyes upon the road.

Seeing the children reminded Jomar of his first
trip to Ur. When he was a little boy, his father had
taken him to the great temple to watch the ceremonies that greeted the new year. He remembered
his father's comforting hand on his shoulder as they
walked toward the city. Like the fragment of a long-
ago dream, he recalled the splendor of the celebration, the sacrifice of a great bull with gold-tipped
horns, and the throngs of joyous people. He looked
around him. Now weary travelers on the road were
seeking relief from their failing farms.

Zefa brought Jomar out of his reverie. "What
food did they give us last night?"

Jomar untied the food pouch and they greedily

ate the smelly goat cheese, briny olives, and two wrinkled plums. They cracked open the husks of pistachio nuts with their teeth and spit out the empty shells as they walked.

The meal was meager. To distract himself from his persistent hunger, Jomar searched the land stretching far ahead. "Zefa, look!" he said, coming to a halt. In the heat-hazed distance, the tan-colored earth rose up from the flat plain and took the shape of a mud-brick wall that wrapped itself around the city. "This is the wall that guards the temple of the moongod and all the wealth of Ur."

They started walking again, but the strained expression on Zefa's thin face returned, and her feet dragged. Others on the dusty road began to pass them.

"Walk faster!" Jomar told her impatiently. "Everyone must speak to the gatekeeper to see if they can enter the city. We don't want to lose our place."

As they neared the wall, Zefa pointed to a group of tattered men, women, and children clustered close to it. "They're not waiting in line. What are they doing there?"

"Wait, I'll find out," Jomar said.

Coming closer, he found crude shelters huddled against the wall that offered some protection from the blistering sun, but no privacy. Jomar spoke with a gaunt man with sad eyes who told him they were offering themselves as slaves in return for food and a place to sleep.

Jomar returned to Zefa. "They're hoping to be hired by those who live inside the city," he told her.

Zefa clutched his arm. "Promise me you'll stay with me no matter what happens."

Jomar peered at his sister's frightened face. "I promise."

Aware of other travelers trying to pass them, Jomar steered Zefa toward the small kiosk that bulged out from the wall. Inside was the man who determined the fate of all who would enter the city.

The sun bore down as they stood in the long, snaking line of people. Children grew quarrelsome with waiting. The odor of anxious, exhausted travelers merged with the sweat of burdened donkeys. From the front of the slowly moving line, angry or pleading voices could be heard, but not the words of the gatekeeper.

"Let me in—my whole family starves in the countryside!"

"I'm a skilled carpenter, and my wife's an excellent cook."

"Unfair! The city depends on us for food, but abandons us when times are bad."

Jomar and Zefa were almost at the gatehouse. How many people were getting in? From the steady stream of dazed and stony faces being turned away, not many.

"Who are you, and what is your business in Ur?" the gatekeeper asked in a droning voice as they finally stood before him.

Jomar straightened his shoulders. "I'm Jomar, son of Durabi. My father made an arrangement with a goldsmith who works for the temple. I'm to be his new apprentice."

The man gestured toward the gate. "Then enter." He looked at Zefa. "And this young girl?"

Zefa's strong fingers gripped Jomar's arm.

"She's my sister," Jomar said in a voice that seemed too loud.

The gatekeeper looked at Jomar, narrowed his lips, and waited for him to continue. "And?" he snapped. "Where will she live? What will she do?"

Jomar's tongue seemed stuck to the roof of his parched mouth.

The people behind them grumbled impatiently. "We're waiting—hurry up!" someone called out.

"Speak!" the gatekeeper said.

"My sister . . . my sister's a musician," Jomar stammered.

"We have temple musicians," the man said irritably, "and we don't need any more hungry young players roaming the streets."

Jomar snatched Zefa's lyre from her basket and held it up.

"A toy," the gatekeeper snorted.

"No, not a toy," Zefa said firmly, and took the lyre from Jomar's hand and held it in position.

"This is no place for a concert!" a young man behind them said angrily.

But Zefa moved her fingers over the lyre's strings and began a hymn to the sungod in a breathy, nervous tone:

> *"Moongod Nanna, your son we glorify.*
> *Each dawn you send us Utu in his chariot golden bright*
> *Pulled by four prancing steeds that surge across the sky.*
> *Utu battles darkness to defeat the night—*
> *Bold Utu battles darkness to give us morning light."*

Jomar watched the gatekeeper's scowl of contempt disappear as Zefa's voice steadied and soared as she sang. He heard people murmuring behind them.

"Her music honors Utu," a strong voice rang out. "Let her in."

The gatekeeper leaned toward Jomar and spoke in a troubled whisper. "I could lose my position if the temple officials find out what I've done, but I'll allow your sister to enter the city. You must not speak of her skills to anyone, lest she be pressed to join one of the bands of music-making beggars." He gestured with his thumb toward the open gates. "Go—but keep her safe, off the streets!"

10 CITY MADE OF MUD

Pulling Zefa behind him, Jomar almost danced with relief as they walked toward the gateway. "You were brave to sing for the gatekeeper! I would never have thought to ask you to do that."

"I know—that's why I decided to sing my song," Zefa said quietly.

As they moved through the immense wooden doors, Jomar wondered where the timber came from and how it got here. The noises of the city—loud cries, snatches of music, the hum of conversation, the scrape of wooden cart wheels—came from every direction. People of all ages and manner of dress surged around them.

Staring at an elegant woman, Zefa stopped and stood rooted. The woman wore a tight gown that left one shoulder bare, and her coiled braids were wound twice around her head. When they were jostled by impatient people trying to get around them, Jomar grasped Zefa's arm again and moved her forward.

The delicious scent of onions and spices filled the air, as well as the more pungent odors of raw fish and mutton. Jomar and Zefa stood on tiptoe to see over the crush of milling people. Stalls and tables were jammed into the slender shadow of the city's wall, and a boundless array of goods lay spread out on the tables or hung from hooks.

"Pierced shells to decorate your finest clothes! Ivory buttons and pearls from the sea sold here!" a vendor shouted.

"I've never seen pearls before," Zefa whispered to Jomar. "They glisten like little moons!"

"My final offer," a gruff voice rang out from the crowd. "I'll give you half your asking price for five buttons I doubt are really ivory."

Another vendor spoke in a coaxing tone. "Here's a lapis lazuli necklace to bring joy to your wife."

Zefa gazed at the strange blue beads flecked with yellow that the merchant held up high. "How Mother would love that necklace," she said.

A high-pitched woman's voice cried out, "The

sweetest honey-baked cakes and the best barley bread in Ur are here!"

Jomar's stomach rumbled. There was so much food here! Had all the grain, all the honey, all the meat come from the countryside where farmers starved? When Zefa reached out toward the loaves of bread stacked on a table, the vendor impatiently shooed her hand away as if it were a fly. Jomar was stung by this rudeness. Where did the baker think the barley came from? He suddenly saw himself as a young boy. Wet with sweat, he ran behind his father's plow to remove clods of dirt from the new furrows so that the tender barley seeds could sprout.

Leaving the baker, they heard tinny music. A small band of thin, raggedy children were playing a lute, rattles, a reed pipe, and a tambourine. When Zefa stopped to listen, they gathered in front of her to sing and play a lively tune that repeated two strong beats followed by a pause.

At the end of the song, the boy with the tambourine turned it over and held it out. Close to tears, Zefa said, "I've nothing to give you." The children's gaunt faces fell, then they scurried away.

"Come on," Jomar said briskly. "We should find the goldsmith's house as soon as possible."

Zefa dragged her feet. "I won't be welcome there."

"You'll get a meal, at least," Jomar said.

"And then?" Zefa asked, her voice trailing off.

"And then I don't know," Jomar sighed. "Father told me Sidah and his wife live in back of the temple. We must be close to it," he said with forced conviction. He hurried Zefa along, careful to keep out of the way of bustling people and laden donkeys.

They came upon a bridge that was crowded with people looking down at a large canal at the bottom of steep earthen walls. Even from a distance, they could sense the excitement of those people packed together on the bridge. Coming closer, they heard fragments of conversation.

"Killing a free man is serious," a prosperous-looking man said. "Better if he'd been a slave."

A shabbily dressed young man responded, "Slave or free, let him drown if he's guilty."

A mother holding her baby spoke up. "He says he didn't do it, so let the river decide."

Hearing the animated talk, Zefa shuddered. "I don't want to go any closer."

"Then stay here," Jomar said. "I'm going to find out what's happening."

He spoke briefly to a woman carrying a basket of dried fish, then returned to Zefa.

"A man charged with killing another man will be thrown into the canal," Jomar said. "If he comes to the surface and manages to get out of the canal, he'll be judged innocent. If he drowns, they believe that he's guilty." He shook his head. "I've never heard of such a cruel custom."

Zefa looked sharply at him. "You sound like you don't believe in the test." When Jomar didn't answer her challenge, she sighed and let him lead her away from the bridge.

The next street they tried was a jumble of mud-colored brick houses and shops. Most of the buildings were squat, like their own farmhouse, but they walked by a two-storied house with jutting balconies that was surrounded by fruit trees and flowering bushes. Zefa slowed down. "This looks like a palace from one of the stories that Mother used to tell me—all about the adventures of god-kings." Her voice trembled. "I want to go home."

Jomar took Zefa's arm. "Keep walking."

Disoriented and hungry, they wandered through the streets of the city until they stood in front of the temple. It was far larger and more complex than Jomar remembered and so sprawling it looked like a city within a city. Pillars and buttresses soared out of the tawny earth. Mud-brick walls gleamed with small cones of black, red, and white that formed precise patterns of zigzags, spirals, and triangles. Confident people dressed in linen and sheepskin climbed the stairs toward huge wooden double doors.

"This is where the moongod lives," Jomar said. "His home is grander than any palace from one of Mother's stories."

As they circled the temple, they found clusters of mud-brick houses and shops jammed against the temple walls and one another. Jomar stopped a man leading a donkey piled with pottery. "Do you know where the goldsmith Sidah lives?"

"Never heard of him," the man said. When three

more people gave Jomar the same answer, Jomar grasped how big the city was. The people in his village would have known the name and whereabouts of everyone who lived there or in the surrounding farms.

Jomar kept asking about Sidah until an old woman wordlessly pointed out a small brick house on the narrow street that looked the same as all the others. When they got closer, Jomar saw that the design of a tool had been deeply etched into a brick placed above the door. It was a tool he was unfamiliar with. This must be the mark of a goldsmith.

The door to the house was open. They could smell cooked cabbage and onions. With Zefa clutching his arm, Jomar stepped over the threshold.

11 THE GOLDSMITH'S HOUSE

The small, dark room they entered was mercifully cooler than the sunbaked streets. A man and a woman sat silently eating their midday meal at a small wooden table.

"Are you Sidah?" Jomar asked, bowing his head to the lean and graying man who was about the same age as his father.

The man rose and looked somberly at him. "I've been waiting for you, Jomar, son of Durabi." He turned to Zefa. "But who is this?"

Jomar hesitated, then took Zefa's hand and brought her forward. "Zefa, my sister." Sidah and his wife said nothing, but Jomar knew by their narrowed eyes that they were displeased. Jomar spoke to the woman, hoping she might be as kindhearted as his mother. "There's not enough food on the farm to feed us all, so at the last moment my father decided to send her with me." Sidah's wife stared coldly at Zefa, so he appealed to the goldsmith. "I beg you, let her stay here until she finds work."

Sidah shook his head forcefully. "Durabi didn't speak of a daughter. He and I had an agreement. She wasn't a part of it."

Sidah's wife rose from her chair. "This house is small, our food supplies meager."

The goldsmith's expression softened. "Nari, look how thin and worn these children are. Feed and house this girl tonight. Tomorrow she'll go."

"They're dirty," Nari said. "They'll eat when they've bathed and changed their clothes." Motioning curtly that Jomar and Zefa should follow her, she led them outside to a tiny mud-brick shed next to the house. On the clay floor rested a jug of water, a cake of strong-smelling tallow and ash soap, and a heavy, long-handled reed brush. "Come back when you've scrubbed yourselves clean."

In the washroom Zefa spoke in a low tone. "Did you see how she looks at me? I'm a stranger to her, yet she hates me!"

"Yes, she's unfriendly—to both of us," Jomar said. "But you're being allowed to stay the night."

"That was the goldsmith's decision, not hers." Zefa took off her tunic and began to scrub herself vigorously in angry, exaggerated movements. "This house is too quiet. Don't they have children?"

"Only one child, a boy my age." Jomar took the soap and brush that Zefa handed him. "He died recently. I'm here to take his place."

"As their son?" Zefa said indignantly. "You have a father and mother."

"I mean his place as Sidah's apprentice," Jomar said quietly. He fingered his shabby tunic. "Without my basket, I have no change of clothing."

"Scrub yourself and leave your tunic on your cot before you go to sleep," Zefa said. "I'll find a way to wash it." From her basket, she took out her one clean garment and put it on. Then, with a private half smile, she circled her braids twice around her head.

When they returned to the house, Sidah invited them to the table with a quick gesture. Without a glance or smile, Nari put down two bowls of soup. Following Zefa's lead, Jomar did not gulp down his food. The meal disappeared in moments, but Nari did not offer them a second serving.

Jomar saw that the goldsmith was looking at him with sad eyes. *He's wishing his son sat at the table instead of me,* Jomar thought, wondering if a sickness had caused his death.

Sidah gave a little shudder as if to throw off his thoughts and rose from the table. "Come, I'll get you started." Without waiting for Jomar to follow him, he disappeared into another room that opened off from the living quarters.

The goldsmith's wife spoke to Zefa directly for the first time. "You've no right to be here, so you'll have to work for me to earn your keep until you leave tomorrow. Clear the table, pick over the lentils, then boil them for tomorrow's meal." She left the table and went outside.

Jomar had seen his sister's eyes harden as she listened to Nari. In one swift motion Zefa loosened her crown of braids.

"Why did you do that?" Jomar said. "I liked your braids piled high."

"Because I'm a slave, not a lady!" she said angrily.

Jomar put a finger to his lips. "Lower your voice—they don't know you're a slave. Remember, you're better off cooking for her instead of for Malak and his crew."

Zefa stacked the bowls on the table with abrupt movements. Jomar started off for the workshop.

12 SIDAH'S WORKSHOP

Determined not to be impressed by anything he saw, Jomar threw back his shoulders and stepped into a small, whitewashed room. He looked coolly about him. The workshop was dimly lit by three small, high windows. Two worktables took up most of the space. Jomar thought the small beehive-shaped furnace on the floor looked like his mother's oven for baking bread. Also on the floor were a blow-pipe to get a fire going, a basket of charcoal, a bowl full of water, and a flat stone worn smooth. Various tools of different shapes and sizes hung from hooks on the wall. Some were familiar, but most were strange to him.

He pointed to an elegant tool that stood out from the others. "Isn't that the same tool that's carved into the brick over your door?"

Sidah nodded. "They're tongs, mainly used to hold heated gold."

Tongs to hold gold! Excited in spite of his resolve, Jomar knew he had entered another world.

Something large and slender stood covered with a cotton cloth in one corner, but Jomar's eye was drawn to three small clay bowls that sat on a worktable. In them were blue, red, and black stones. He pointed to the blue ones. "A merchant in the bazaar this morning called these lapis lazuli."

"Did he?" Sidah asked in a skeptical tone. "You can't believe everything you hear in the city. The temple controls the lapis we import to make sacred objects and jewelry for important people. The gems are so costly and difficult to obtain that they are rarely sold on the streets. The beads you saw were probably fakes made of clay and painted blue to look like lapis."

Jomar felt like the farm boy he was. "Where do the real ones come from?"

Sidah's voice took on a teaching tone as he pointed to the three clay bowls in turn. "Merchants travel over deserts or up snowy mountains to bring back red carnelian, black obsidian, and fine blue lapis. We have no splendid gems or gold, tin, or copper in this land. We lack stone quarries and even timber."

"Where did the wood of the great gate of Ur come from?" Jomar asked.

"Huge logs from the northern mountains are roped together and floated down the river," Sidah answered.

Jomar thought of the effort that must go into supplying the city with everything it needed or wanted. "A merchant's life must be hard."

Sidah nodded. "Hard and risky. But if a trader returns with valuable goods, he can become rich, build a grand house, own many slaves. But he can lose everything to bandits, including his life. Sometimes the donkeys that pull his caravans die of thirst or exhaustion. Or his richly laden boats may overturn in the river or the sea. . . ." Sidah's eyes clouded over and he stopped talking.

Jomar waited for him to continue. When he didn't, he asked another question. "What does the city trade for these foreign goods?"

"Oil and spices, woven cotton and wool, and the

tools and weapons we make from imported metal," Sidah answered. "But mostly we trade with the surplus grain that's piled up in temple storehouses."

"Surplus grain?" Jomar said, his voice rising. "In this drought, what grain is surplus when those who live in the countryside go hungry?"

Sidah shook his head. "You're not going to change the way the temple conducts its business. Farmers and merchants must contribute their produce to the temple so that its staff is fed. It's also used for trade." Sidah spoke sternly. "The city lives on trade and would wither without it."

Jomar was stung by Sidah's reproach. He said nothing, but his mind was filled with images of sun-baked barren fields, the bony cow, her hungry calf.

Sidah picked up a thin rod of gold that was almost as tall as Zefa. One end of the rod turned up at a sharp angle. "I've just finished this drinking straw for a high-ranking priestess."

Jomar took the rod that Sidah held out to him. "This is so light!"

Sidah nodded. "Inside is a hollow reed I've covered with gold foil no thicker than a moth's wing.

Temple officials like to drink beer together out of a deep urn." He took back the tube and briefly put one end to his mouth. "This reaches below the impurities that form on the surface of the brew."

"I thought spitting out bits of barley husks was part of beer drinking," Jomar said.

Sidah had a hint of a smile on his face. "Important people don't like to spit."

Jomar grinned. "How do you get the gold, the gemstones, your tools?"

Sidah swept the room with his hand. "The temple provides me with a steady supply of the materials to make whatever those at the temple need—or think they need."

Jomar pointed to the long drinking rod. "Except for this, I see little gold."

Sidah's expression hardened. "Gold is far too rare and valuable to be kept here. Thieves will risk everything to obtain it."

Jomar knew Sidah would view him with suspicion until he could prove to him he could be trusted.

Sidah waved a hand around the room. "You've had a long journey, but I want to get you started with your training. One of your daily tasks will be to keep the workshop swept clean. The oven must be kept clear of ashes and the coals banked at the back of the oven to retain their heat. At the end of the day the tools must be returned to the wall and hung on the same hooks. You must know each tool and its function."

"Some are new to me. . . ." Jomar murmured.

Sidah nodded. "I'll touch each tool, name it, and describe how it's used. After I'm finished, you'll repeat what I've told you."

Slowly and methodically, Sidah went through every tool that hung from the wall. Then it was Jomar's turn, and he started off well. He pointed to familiar tools, such as hammers and knives, and described their function. But halfway through his assignment he began to falter. When the name of the tool or its function escaped him, Jomar stammered. His pauses got longer and longer. *The goldsmith must think he made a foolish agreement with my father.*

Sidah held his palm up and stopped the lesson. "You have little knowledge of this craft, but if you're clever you'll find out what you must know by watching me." He changed the subject abruptly. "Your sister is a worry for us all. Where will she seek work?"

"I'm not sure," Jomar answered. "She's good with farm animals . . . collecting dung for fire fuel . . . spinning wool. . . ." He trailed off, determined to honor the gatekeeper's warning not to speak of Zefa's musical skills to anyone.

"Those are country chores," Sidah said. "Ur is over-run with farm and village people in need of work."

"Yes," Jomar said faintly. "We saw many of them on the road."

Sidah shook his head. "The city is full of peril for a young country girl. She must find employment soon. Otherwise you'll be forced to give up this apprenticeship in order to find her a secure place to live and earn her way."

Jomar was startled. *Leave my apprenticeship before it begins?* He imagined himself and Zefa wandering the city, hungry and homeless. Or worse—joining the people outside the city walls who were offering themselves as slaves in order to survive. A terrible weariness overcame him. Beneath the fatigue was fear.

13 A BARGAIN STRUCK

"Nari," Sidah called to his wife. "Give us an early supper. These children need rest." He and Jomar left the workshop.

Zefa served a simple meal of cucumbers, onions, and tomatoes before sitting down with the others. Jomar was so tired he thought he might fall asleep at the table.

"You've invited the girl to stay the night," Nari said to her husband. "Where's she supposed to sleep?"

"The workroom," Sidah answered. "It's always empty at night."

"We've no extra cot," Nari said. "She'll have to sleep on the floor."

Sidah turned to Jomar. "After Zefa cleans up, Nari will get her settled in the workroom. I'll show you where you'll sleep."

A wide reed bench separated the sleeping quarters

from the kitchen area. Behind the bench were three wooden cots with mattresses of braided reed lacing. When Sidah bent down to tenderly touch the folded cotton blankets on one of the cots, Jomar knew this had been his son's bed.

"I'm going out to a little shop near here where craftsmen gather," Sidah said quietly. "I need to be with my old friends for a while."

Friends, Jomar said wistfully to himself. His farm was located far from the nearest village, and the long workday left him no time to be with people other than his family. He wanted friends, but how would he be able to make them here in the city?

The long day was finally turning into night. Spreading one blanket over the cot's reed lacing, Jomar sat down on the bed and took off his tunic. He covered himself with the other blanket and left his tunic on top of it. Humming Zefa's lullaby under his breath, Jomar was asleep in moments.

He awoke in darkness. From the workshop came the low thrum of a lyre, a lyre with deep and haunting tones. For a brief moment the individual notes wove themselves into a small tapestry of patterns, then stopped. Faint echoes of music hung in the air before disappearing entirely.

I'm dreaming, Jomar said to himself.

Then he heard the stirrings of Nari and Sidah and their drowsy, half-formed conversation.

"What is it?"

"That music . . ."

"In the workshop."

"The lyre . . . "

"Who . . . ?"

Nari got out of bed. "I'm going to thrash that girl!"

Jomar sprang up from his cot. "Don't hurt her!" Wrapping a blanket around his waist, he stumbled toward the workshop.

Nari was ahead of him. "She searched that room like a common thief, took the covering off the lyre, and played on it!"

Sidah lit an oil lamp and held it high as he entered the workshop. Its glow caught Zefa cowering on the floor next to a tall lyre whose cloth cover lay puddled at her feet.

Jomar thrust himself protectively in front of Zefa, but Nari moved toward her as if he were invisible.

"Nari, leave her be!" Sidah shouted. "You're right. She shouldn't have touched the lyre. But didn't you hear the music she made?"

As if struck, Nari stopped moving.

Sidah turned toward Jomar. "Who taught her to play like that?"

"I—I made a small lyre for her when she was little," Jomar stammered. "She taught herself how to play it."

Sidah spoke in a faraway voice. "I've never heard the music this lyre can make. Beautiful sounds, rich tones. The gods have sent me a sign."

Nari's head jerked up. "A sign? What sign?"

Sidah gave no indication that he'd heard either Nari's question or Zefa's soft weeping. He sat down heavily at the table. "Last year Kurgal, the temple music director, had me come to the temple to see an extraordinary lyre that had been created by temple craftsmen. My assignment was to embellish this instrument."

"Embellish?" Jomar asked in a small voice.

"Yes, embellish—to decorate it in such a way that the lyre would be more splendid than any known," Sidah said.

"It was a great honor to have been chosen," Nari interrupted.

Again Sidah ignored her. "I looked forward to working on it with my son, Abban, already a skilled craftsman. We went to the temple frequently to examine the lyre. We discussed our ideas for its embellishment endlessly—" He broke off and rubbed his eyes with the back of his hands. "Abban died before we were to begin."

Jomar thought this might be the right time to ask his question. "How—how did Abban die?"

Sidah did not speak for a moment. "I sent my son to inspect a shipment of carnelian gems on a trading boat anchored out in the harbor," he finally said. "The gems were bound for the temple, so they had to be of the finest quality." He looked up, pride in his eyes. "My boy was a good judge of gems." He paused again. "Metal tools crated for export were foolishly hauled onto the boat before they'd taken off large stones that were coming into the city for temple statuary. The boat wasn't built to withstand such a heavy load. It sank."

"And your son drowned," Jomar said quietly.

Nari's body seemed to cave in upon itself on hearing Jomar's whispered words.

With an effort, Sidah went on. "I did not have the heart to work on the lyre without Abban. I went to Kurgal and urged him to give the assignment to another goldsmith. He refused to do so, and had the lyre strung so it could be played at the coming new year celebration without my embellishment. Then Kurgal— always so sympathetic—had a sudden change of heart. He threatened me with the loss of my temple position if I refused to complete the lyre in time for the ceremony. When I reluctantly agreed, he immediately had the lyre brought to my workshop."

Sidah sat in his chair without moving, then spoke in a thick voice. "I agreed because I thought I would not be able to withstand the loss of both my son and my occupation." He rose and entered the workshop to speak gently to Zefa, still huddled on the floor. "The gods have brought you here to let me hear the glorious tones of the lyre. You will inspire me as I work on it."

Nari broke in. "No! Only temple musicians are allowed to play that instrument!"

Sidah dismissed what she said with a cutting gesture. "I will hear Zefa play on it only for a short while. After we start the gold work, it can't be played."

Nari shook her head in disbelief. "Your new apprentice is a farm boy who knows nothing, nothing! Now you would open this house to another ignorant young stranger from the country? Someone who dares to touch the temple lyre?" Her voice was raspy. "If the girl stays, she'll work for me."

Sidah's lips tightened. "And when I ask her, she'll play for me."

A bargain had been struck, but Jomar's only thought was that Zefa would be safe for as long as she lived here. "Thank you," he said to Sidah. He grasped Zefa's hand, prompting her.

Zefa stood. "Thank you," she echoed.

"You'll do my bidding, so don't think you'll lead an easy life of music making," Nari said. "On the day the lyre is finished, you'll go."

Jomar caught a flash of resentment in Zefa's eyes and squeezed her hand in warning. This house was now his sister's refuge, a walled sanctuary within a city full of dangers.

"Enough talk—we'll sleep," Sidah said. "Tomorrow will be a long workday."

14 NECKLACE FOR A HIGH PRIESTESS

Jomar awoke to find his only garment, still damp, spread out on his blanket. Zefa had kept her word despite the turbulent night. At home, his dirty tunic would have been washed by his mother, not his sister.

He got up and dressed quickly. In the cooking area Zefa was preparing wheat porridge for the morning meal. Nari hovered near her, clucking and giving orders. "We don't serve plain mush in this house. Add nuts and honey for flavor."

When Zefa put a steaming bowl in front of him, Jomar saw that her hands were shaking. He looked up at her, pointed to his tunic, and nodded his thanks. She smiled weakly.

Sidah beckoned to Jomar from the workroom.

Quickly swallowing down his porridge, Jomar left the kitchen.

He looked at the shrouded lyre with new eyes, but it seemed they were not going to work on it today. Instead Sidah took down a wooden tray from a high shelf and put it on one of the worktables. A dozen small, delicately veined leaves of gold lay in a circle on the tray. Lapis beads alternated with those of translucent red carnelian inside the ring of gold leaves.

Sidah bent to gently blow away dust that had settled over the beads. "The high priestess Bittatti ordered this necklace some time ago. Abban worked on it and wanted to do the stringing himself. I put it away when he died, but now you will do it. I don't see as well as I used to, but your eyes are young and keen—as his were. I'll get you started."

Sitting at the worktable with Jomar, Sidah held up a length of thin, rolled sheep gut, then ran one end of it along a small cake of beeswax. "This makes the threading easier." Squinting and holding a carnelian bead close to his face, he worked the thread through the hole in the bead, then repeated the process with two lapis beads. "Next comes a gold leaf—lapis and gold go well together. The leaves are delicate—handle them carefully. Repeat the pattern until the necklace is complete and secure."

Jomar pointed toward the three bowls that held the unworked gems. "How do rough stones like that turn into these perfect beads?"

"Someday I'll show you how it's done, but now you'll string the necklace." Sidah placed Jomar in front of the tray, then went over to the lyre and removed its cloth covering.

Jomar gasped. In the darkness of the night, he had seen almost nothing of the lyre. He thought it would be an unadorned wood and gut-stringed instrument. Instead it was as tall as Zefa. On a panel in front of the lyre there were four lively scenes made with inlaid shell depicting human and animal figures.

"But it's already decorated," Jomar said. "What more is needed?"

"You'll see, you'll see," Sidah said impatiently. He slid the lyre to a sunny spot and began to examine the instrument with such concentration that Jomar felt that he was alone in the workroom.

With an act of will, Jomar made himself turn his attention to the task of stringing the necklace. He worked slowly, trying to imitate Sidah's smooth, sure movements. Halfway through his assignment, he studied his calloused hands, still covered with cuts from his work at the reservoir. He couldn't believe a farmer's son was shaping the delicate piece in front of him.

Jomar worked on, finally needing only one more lapis bead to complete the necklace. *It wasn't on the tray!* Furtively he bent down to search the floor, but it had been swept clean. His mind leapt. Zefa had spent the night in the workroom. Alone. Could she have taken the bead? With a jolt Jomar remembered the merchant in the bazaar holding up a strand of blue beads. "How Mother would love that necklace," Zefa had said. Was she secretly planning to return to the farm with a lavish gift for their mother?

Jomar could hear the beating of his heart. "What if there aren't enough gold leaves—or beads—to maintain the pattern?" he asked Sidah quietly.

Sidah looked up, frowning. "Part of a goldsmith's job is to work that out before beginning something new. Why do you ask?"

Jomar tried to keep the panic out of his voice. "One lapis bead is missing. . . ." His words dried up, but he was aware of the sweat on his body.

Sidah came to the worktable and stared at the tray, his lips compressed into a straight line. "You'll learn how to make a bead sooner than I thought," he snapped.

With abrupt motions, Sidah selected a piece of lapis from the clay bowl and steadied it between wood pincers that were attached to the table. Then he poured abrasive sand on top of the gemstone. Picking up what looked like a miniature bow and arrow, he wound the bow string around it. By pushing and pulling the bow, Sidah made the drill spin so fast that its rotations were a blur—like Jomar's mind. He had trouble following what Sidah was doing.

After a short while, Sidah held up the lapis bead for Jomar to see that a narrow hole had been neatly bored through the gem. "After you've polished this with sand and wool, you can complete the necklace," he said coldly.

Jomar found it difficult to meet his gaze. "Now

that we know that a bead is missing, will you count the unworked gems in the clay bowls?"

Sidah's eyes had the piercing gaze of a hawk. "I don't need to. They've been counted. By the temple. And by me."

15 AN ASSIGNMENT

Entering the workshop, Zefa put down two bowls of lentil and barley soup for the midday meal. Her eyes opened wide when she saw the lapis beads with tiny yellow flecks embedded in them. "These blue stones look like small fragments of the starry night sky," she said, putting out a hand as if to touch them. Then her face flushed and she bounded out of the room.

Sidah sat down at the table. "Your sister speaks like a poet."

To Jomar, Zefa's tense, quick movements made her seem like someone with a guilty secret. "She's always making up songs," he said, trying to keep his voice light. "Is this what you mean about being a poet?"

Sidah nodded. "Her words make you see things in a new way. In spite of what's happened, I want to hear her songs played on the temple lyre before she goes."

In spite of what's happened. This was proof that Sidah believed Zefa had taken the bead.

After their meal was finished, Sidah rose and took the drinking straw down from a shelf. "Tomorrow you and I will start working on the lyre. But I want you to deliver this to the high priestess today."

Jomar was startled. "I'm to go alone?"

Sidah's expression was somber. "I have work to do."

Jomar suspected he was being tested. How could he prove to Sidah that he'd made the delivery to the high priestess?

Sidah wrapped the drinking straw in a length of cotton cloth and tied it with a braided strip of leather. The end of the leather strip had been inserted into a lump of clay on which a small design had been impressed.

Jomar touched it. "Why is this bit of clay here?"

Sidah picked up a small cylinder of black stone and showed it to Jomar. "I used this seal to press the design into a moist square of clay."

Jomar had to look intently to see the design carved on the little stone scroll. "Oh, it's people drinking beer. Through long straws!"

"It is," Sidah said. "I've made many gold straws for the temple, so I decided to make that little scene my mark, my symbol." He gave the wrapped package to Jomar. "Walk quickly to the temple. Don't call attention to yourself. Temple staff and craftsmen are allowed to use the back entrance."

"But I'm not really a craftsman," Jomar said. "Will they let me in?"

"Show the guard my seal so he'll know I sent you," Sidah said. "Ask where the chambers of the high priestess are located. Bittatti is powerful and proud. Show her every deference in your gesture and speech. When your task is completed, return home immediately."

Home. Did Sidah truly accept him as a part of his household?

Jomar saw that Sidah was waiting for his response. "I'll do as you say." But his thoughts were in such a jumble that he had to think hard to remember what Sidah had told him. He left the house with the package tucked under his arm.

Zefa was coming toward him carrying a mesh bag filled with fruit and vegetables. *In spite of the drought, the temple managed to feed its staff well,* Jomar thought resent-fully. With a start, he realized that now he was one of those working for the temple.

Nari walked behind Zefa, unburdened. Her eyes darted to the package that Jomar held. "What are you carrying? Where are you going?"

"Sidah is sending me to deliver the drinking straw to the high priestess," Jomar said.

"Too trusting, too soon," she muttered, sweep-ing past him into the house.

Jomar glared at her back, then started off toward the temple. He tried to achieve a relaxed stride and a carefree expression, but the long package was awk-ward and soon drew unwelcome attention.

A boy about his own age came out of the house next door and came up to Jomar. Falling in step with him, the boy casually tossed a ball made from an inflated animal bladder from hand to hand. "You must be the goldsmith's new apprentice," he said.

"I am," Jomar said, increasing his pace.

The boy walked faster to keep up. "My name is Gamil. The goldsmith's son, Abban, was my closest friend." He cleared his throat, but the next words came out in a whisper. "I miss him." He shook his head and hurried on. "Abban was so proud of the work he did on the pieces made in his father's workshop."

Jomar wanted no part of a conversation that could compare his poor skills with Abban's. He shifted the drinking straw to his other arm and looked straight ahead. "I'm sure Abban was well-trained and talented."

Gamil pointed to the package. "I know that Sidah doesn't permit anything to leave the workshop that isn't finished, so you must be taking something to the temple, probably something wonderful. Am I right?"

Why did he want to know? Hadn't Sidah warned him to be wary of city people? "I have a delivery to make and no time to talk."

Gamil's shoulders fell, and he dropped back.

Free of Gamil, Jomar abandoned his effort to appear competent and in control. He grasped his package firmly and hurried on with his head down. Nearing the back of the temple, he stopped short to avoid running into a tall man with a protruding stomach who seemed to have deliberately put himself in his way. Jomar looked up.

Malak!

The lips of the temple official were twisted into the same superior half smile that Jomar loathed. "Ah, the farm boy. I've been looking for you. Didn't you say you would be apprenticing with a goldsmith named Sidah?" Malak reached out and grasped Jomar's free arm. "You must be carrying something valuable."

"Let me be," Jomar said. "I have business to conduct in the temple."

Malak exerted more pressure. "Such a responsible job for one who ran away from his responsibilities."

Jomar tried to appear confident. "I'm not your slave," he said, and instantly regretted using the word.

"You're not, but your sister is," Malak said. "She's not only a slave, but something more serious. A runaway slave. Do you know the penalties slaves receive for escaping?"

Jomar thought of Qat-nu's wounds, and his stomach twisted into a knot. "I'm sure they're severe."

"Oh, yes." Malak's grip dug into Jomar's arm. "Branding. Flogging. And worse. I, too, am on my way to the temple to receive my next assignment. I'll find out where your goldsmith lives and soon come calling. I'm sure he'll be interested in knowing more about his new apprentice and his young sister." Malak flung open the back door of the temple and disappeared.

Only the task that Sidah had given him prevented Jomar from sliding into a numbing despair.

16 IN BITTATTI'S CHAMBER

Jomar waited outside the temple until he was sure Malak was occupied receiving his next assignment. He secured his package and opened the temple door. He looked around nervously—Malak was not there. Jomar entered a vast and peaceful space. The white-washed ceiling and walls were broken up by shadows cast by columns and jutting buttresses that support-ed the clay-brick structure. Jomar found some relief from his troubles in the cool, quiet sanctuary.

This serenity was disturbed when a man stepped forward. "What's your business here?"

Jomar knew he must turn all his attention to his assignment. "With your permission, I'm to deliver this to the high priestess Bittatti," Jomar said, hold-ing out his package for inspection.

The man fingered the seal. "Ah, you're fortunate to have been chosen as Sidah's new apprentice. Go outside and enter by the front of the temple, because the chambers of the high priestess are located there. A young handmaiden guards her door." His face grew grave, and he shook his finger in warning. "Once inside her chambers, do not linger after your delivery has been completed."

Jomar nodded. He walked outside and entered the great temple through the imposing double doors. Inside he passed dozens of rooms, and through open doors he caught glimpses of court-yards and rooms behind rooms. Finally he came upon a young woman who stood in front of a carved wooden door. A simple necklace of one lapis bead hugged her throat. He thought of Zefa.

Jomar held up his package to the handmaiden. "The high priestess, Bittatti, waits for this. The goldsmith Sidah has instructed me to give it to your mistress."

The young woman smiled. "I'll lead you to her."

Jomar followed her into a room filled with light and patterns. Woven textiles with strong geometric designs covered the walls and floor. Then he saw a woman so still that he thought for a moment that she was a statue. She was seated on a high-backed wooden chair embellished with inlaid shell. The legs of the chair were carved to look like those of a lion. The high priestess had the self-assured stare of a lioness at rest.

Bittatti's gown was made of tasseled sheepskin that left one shoulder bare, but it was her jewelry that astonished him. Large gold earrings shaped like crescent moons hung to her shoulders. Gold leaves wreathed her head, similar to the ones in the necklace he was stringing. Had Sidah also made this dazzling jewelry?

Bittatti's only movement was the impatient drumming of her fingers on the arm of her chair. Jomar bowed and handed her the package. "I bring you this from the goldsmith Sidah."

The high priestess unwrapped the parcel and examined the drinking straw carefully, then lightly touched her golden crown of leaves and her crescent earrings. "Sidah's work is superior to all others," she said in an authoritative voice, then turned to her handmaiden. "Give him the contract tablet."

The young woman handed Jomar a hard clay

rectangle that was smaller than his palm and covered with evenly spaced markings. What was this tablet? He was uncertain what to do or say.

"I think you have never seen the written word," Bittatti said coolly.

Jomar nodded in baffled agreement.

"You hold in your hands a record of my assignment to Sidah," she said. "Take it to him. The temple keeps a duplicate tablet here."

So that was why Sidah had trusted him with the drinking straw. The tablet would be proof of his delivery to the high priestess.

Jomar stared at the clay piece in his hand. "Who made this?" Then he worried that he shouldn't be asking Bittatti such a question. Or any question.

The high priestess gazed at him without expression. "There are special rooms in the temple where people called scribes do nothing but make records in clay and carve words on stone to honor our great moongod. The scribes know how to make these wedge-shaped marks and understand their meaning."

Before he could silence himself, Jomar asked, "Can Sidah read what I will bring to him?"

Bittatti shook her head. "It takes many years of difficult study to learn to read and write. Those who can are often made priests of the temple." She sat up even straighter in her chair. "I'm one of the few women who have mastered the discipline."

"You can read this?" Jomar blurted.

The half smile on Bittatti's lips held both pride and scorn. "My older brother received instruction in how to read and write, but he failed to learn. I pleaded to take his place and was finally allowed to do so." She raised her chin. "I dedicated myself to the task and achieved great success."

Jomar was awestruck by this forceful woman, but he knew he should leave. Sidah had told him to show the high priestess courtesy in word and gesture. "You have been kind," Jomar said, bowing low to her.

Bittatti stared at Jomar with intense black eyes made even more striking by their thick black outline. She dismissed him with a nod.

Jomar left her chambers and walked back through the temple. Before this he had seen only graceful, rhythmic designs on the base of stone statues of bearded gods, on huge urns, on walls and columns. Now he knew that these marks were words that had meaning to those who could read them.

17 INNOCENT?

Jomar hurried back to tell Sidah about his meeting with the high priestess, but he was annoyed to find Gamil leaning against the wall of his house as if waiting for him.

"Here again?" Jomar asked. "Don't you have work to do?"

"I work with my father, helping to load and unload the donkeys that merchants send out on trading trips," Gamil answered. "When my father goes on such a journey, I must stay behind to care for my sick mother."

Jomar's cheeks burned in embarrassment for his rudeness. "I'm sorry for your troubles," he said quietly, then turned away to enter Sidah's house.

"No, stay for a moment," Gamil said. "What's your name? Are you from the city? Who is the young girl I see leaving and entering the goldsmith's house?"

"My name is Jomar. I'm from the country, and the girl you see is my sister. Sidah is waiting for me." He left before Gamil could ask any more questions.

On entering the house Jomar heard the sweet sounds of Zefa singing above the humming strings of the great lyre. Unaware of Jomar's presence, Nari sat at the kitchen table listening intently. Was she even breathing? Suddenly she put her hands over her face and quietly wept, her shoulders shaking with her muffled sobs.

Jomar cleared his throat to let her know she was not alone. Startled with surprise, Nari struggled to control her tears. Without acknowledging his presence she rose from the table and busied herself with shelling peas. Jomar quickly left her to enter the workroom.

Sidah sat listening to Zefa with his eyes closed. After she stopped singing, Zefa strummed the lyre for a moment more, then quieted the strings with the palms of her hands. "It must be difficult playing on a lyre of this size, but the sounds you make are beautiful. I will remember your music as I work on the lyre," Sidah said in a gentle voice. With a radiant face Zefa bowed and left the workroom.

When Sidah looked up and saw Jomar, his expression changed. "How can I be so moved by the music of a child who steals from me?" He made a curt, dismissive gesture with his hand. "I'll deal with that when the lyre's completed."

"Thank you for letting Zefa stay until then," Jomar murmured.

Sidah ignored his thanks. "I followed you to the temple to make certain you would make the delivery. Who was that man I saw you talking to near the back entrance?"

Jomar sucked in his breath: he'd been followed! He couldn't risk telling Sidah about Malak. If he knew of Zefa's enslavement and Malak's threat to find her, Zefa would be expelled from the goldsmith's house instantly. And he would be forced to go with her. "He was a man we met on our journey to Ur," he said.

"I've told you, don't trust strangers," Sidah said, then dropped the subject. "How did the high priestess receive the drinking straw?"

Jomar smiled. "She believes your work is the finest of all the temple goldsmiths."

Relief flooded Sidah's face. "It's important that Bittatti thinks well of my skills. I was told she was angry when I refused to embellish the lyre after Abban's death."

Jomar handed the magical clay tablet to Sidah. "The high priestess told me that these marks are all about the golden straw. She knows how to read them, but I don't understand how such information can be captured by just these scratches on this little piece of clay."

"Ah, Bittatti tells everyone that she's one of the few women who can read and write," Sidah said. "I can't make out these scratches, as you call them, but they're a record of my commission to create the drinking straw." Sidah studied the tablet for a moment before carefully putting it in a basket filled with many others. "No mere human could have invented writing. It's a gift from the gods."

"The jewelry you made for the high priestess is beautiful," Jomar said. "Do you think your talent is a gift from the gods as well?"

"No," Sidah said decisively. "My talent is based on years of hard work."

"I know nothing but farming," Jomar said in a subdued tone. "Will I ever be able to create such fine pieces?"

"It will take a long time to determine whether you can or not," Sidah said.

A long time—with no certain results. A wave of yearning for his parents and life on the farm swept over Jomar. He missed his mother's smile. He missed poling his boat on the misty marsh lake in the early morning. And he missed the feel of the wet, slippery skin of a newborn calf.

"Do you know where Zefa went?" Jomar asked with a heavy heart. "I must speak with her."

Sidah's eyes narrowed. "Yes, you must talk to her about the missing bead."

Jomar nodded but had trouble meeting Sidah's steady gaze.

"Nari put her to work washing clothes behind

the house," Sidah said. "I pulled her away to play for me, but I'm sure she's gone back to her chore."

Jomar found his sister on her knees beside a large clay basin. When he approached her Zefa sat back on her heels, letting the wet clothes fall from her hands into the basin. She looked up at him with a smile on her flushed face.

Jomar steeled his heart against her smile. "I've had no time to be alone with you since you played on the temple lyre. Zefa, how could you have done such a foolish thing?"

Her face fell. "I woke up in the middle of the night, uncomfortable where Nari had told me to sleep. When I tried to find a better spot, I brushed up against something tall and heard deep sounds, mysterious sounds. I took off the covering and found a lyre larger than I had ever imagined." She closed her eyes and moved her fingers over invisible strings. "When I touched it, lovely low notes flowed out."

For a moment Zefa's dreamy expression made Jomar want to forget about the missing bead. But he must speak of it. "Zefa, something serious has happened. Something valuable is missing from the workshop. When I was stringing a necklace this morning, I discovered that a lapis bead was gone. What do you know about this?"

Her eyes were wide with surprise. "A bead—a blue bead—missing?"

"Yes. Just one."

"So you think because I played on the temple lyre that I'm a thief as well?"

"You must tell me the truth," Jomar said, his voice rising. "Did you take the bead?"

"I'm your sister!" Zefa cried. "How can you think that of me?"

"You were alone in the workshop all night," Jomar said. "Perhaps you thought you could take the lapis bead and hide it somewhere."

She sprang up and raced inside the house, returning with her reed basket. "Search it!"

Jomar hesitated. Zefa looked at him defiantly and turned the basket upside down at his feet.

He bent down and looked at the meager belongings strewn on the ground, gently touching the little lyre to be sure it wasn't broken. "All right, it's not here," Jomar said. "But if you took it—perhaps to give it to Mother someday—you must return it."

"I can't return something I don't have!"

Jomar was shaken by her righteous anger, but he forced himself to speak in a low, flat voice. "If I find the bead on the tray tomorrow morning, I'll forgive you and try to understand."

"Forgive me? For what? And how could you understand anything that has to do with me?" Zefa's voice rose. "Your only concern is that I should obey Nari's orders and not cause trouble. But you . . . you belong here! While I'm that woman's servant, you're learning the skills of a goldsmith."

Jomar had no answer to her outburst, because what Zefa said was true.

Zefa glared at him defiantly, then returned to scrubbing the wet clothes. She did not look up again.

In the hot glare of the sun, his sister looked young and vulnerable. But was she innocent? Jomar gazed down at her thin shoulders and reached out to touch her. He withdrew his hand, knowing that she would angrily brush it off. Instead of protecting

Zefa, he had become her enemy, her accuser. And there was the threat of Malak. Jomar could not bring himself to tell her of his meeting with him and have her live in terror of his return. Jomar's strength was disappearing. He could not make her confess she'd taken the bead. He did not know how to shield her from Malak.

18 A PUZZLING PIECE

When he returned to the workshop, Sidah stared at him expectantly. "Well, did she take the gem?"

Jomar looked away. "She denies it."

"But it's gone!" Sidah said. Then he clamped his lips together. "Both of us must put aside our suspicions about the bead until the lyre is finished. Embellishing it is my first chance to do important work for the temple since Abban's death."

He abruptly brought down a strange wooden half sphere from a shelf and held it up in front of the lyre's sound box. "What do you think this is?"

Jomar tried to turn his attention to the puzzling piece before him. "I'm not sure . . . I don't know," he said haltingly.

"I didn't expect you to know," Sidah said. "It will be the head of a bull."

"A bull's head? The eyes and ears are missing. The muzzle is strange, and where are the horns?"

"This rough head was made by a temple craftsman, but it's up to me to make the bull look noble," Sidah said. "I'll create a proper nose and mouth, and put in place the eyes, horns, and ears that have been made by other craftmen. This will happen after the head has been sheathed with gold."

"Sheathed with gold?" Jomar echoed. "How?"

Sidah frowned. "You'll see the process as we work. While we wait for the temple to deliver what we need, Bittatti's necklace must be finished." He took up a bit of wool and a small bowl of sand and showed Jomar how to polish the new lapis bead. As Jomar worked to bring the bead to the same sheen as the missing one, images of Zefa's angry face and Malak's scowl flitted through his mind like small flying insects.

When Jomar thought his task was finished, he got down the tray that held the necklace. Placing the bead he had polished next to the others, Jomar brought the tray to Sidah. "Is the new one a good match?" he asked nervously.

Sidah compared the new lapis bead with the

ones in the necklace, and grunted his approval. "And now the stringing," he said.

Grateful for a task he was sure he could do, Jomar completed the necklace, and again brought the tray to Sidah.

"Finally it's finished," Sidah said. "It's taken too long——" He broke off when two men strode into the workshop without warning or word of greeting.

From their air of authority, Jomar knew that they were from the temple. The tall, muscled younger man seemed to be a guard, his hand never leaving the dagger at his waist. The gray-haired man hugged a wooden box close to his chest. Opening the box, he put a handful of small nuggets of bright metal on a worktable. "Sidah, you now have the material for the work I've ordered you to do." His words were commanding, but they were spoken in a soft voice.

Jomar thrust himself forward to look. "Gold," he said under his breath.

Sidah shot him a disapproving glance. The guard glared at him. The man who had brought the gold raised his eyebrows and looked at Sidah.

"My new apprentice," Sidah said evenly. "Jomar,

this is Kurgal, the temple's music director." Jomar nodded and slipped back into the shadows.

Kurgal did not acknowledge Jomar, but handed Sidah a clay tablet covered with rows of the wedge-shaped marks. "As you know, this is the contract for your work on the lyre and a record of the weight of the gold I've delivered to you." He gazed somberly at the goldsmith. "I'm mindful that you are without the help of your talented son, but you must work quickly. This lyre will be the most important instrument in the coming new year celebration."

Sidah bowed his head. "You've been patient with me. I give you my assurance the lyre will be finished in time."

Kurgal nodded and gestured to his guard to follow him, and the two men left the workshop.

Sidah spoke with an odd mixture of pride and sorrow in his voice. "And so our task begins."

Our task. Jomar could feel a small bubble of excitement rising within him. The bull's head would be sheathed with gold!

19 SHEET OF GOLD

After the men left, Jomar was surprised to see Sidah cover the necklace with cloth and put it on a high shelf. "I'm not to take it to the high priestess?" Jomar asked.

"We have a great deal to do and time is short," Sidah said. "Bittatti will have her necklace when the lyre is completed. Now our day will begin when the sungod returns to the morning sky and lightens this room. When his chariot disappears and darkness comes, we'll eat and sleep."

This was a familiar pattern to Jomar. In the hot season, his family rose before the sun in order to do as much work as possible before the heat of the day drained their energies. *His family.* He had never missed them more or been so unsure of himself. Again he thought of the weak newborn calf. Had it survived beyond its difficult first night?

Sidah pointed to the furnace, then to the blow-pipe. "Bring the coals back to life."

Grateful for another task that he could do, Jomar stirred the coals and blew on them with the blowpipe. "Are you going to melt the gold before you begin to work on it?" Jomar asked when the little furnace had warmed.

"No, melting is only done when gold is poured into a mold," Sidah said. "But as the work progresses, I may have to heat the gold from time to time to keep it from becoming too brittle."

"How can you tell when it needs heating?" Jomar asked.

"The gold will tell me—I'll feel its resistance when I hammer," Sidah said. "Don't look so worried. Gold is a soft, pliant metal, and forgiving if a mistake is made."

Do goldsmiths make mistakes? Jomar felt that he was being given secret information that only real craftsmen knew.

Sidah put a thin piece of leather on the flat stone, put the gold nuggets on top, then covered them with another piece of leather. He dropped to his knees and began to pound the gold with a small wooden mallet with vigorous, rhythmic strokes.

After a while he took off the top piece of leather. "Look, the gold is beginning to flatten and fuse." Sidah continued hammering for a long time, then stopped. "The gold tells me it needs heat." He pointed to a bowl full of water and indicated that Jomar should move it close to the brick furnace. Sidah transferred the gold to a clay tray and thrust it inside the furnace with the tongs. He left it there until it began to turn red. Then in a quick, smooth motion, he plunged the gold into the bowl, where it made a satisfying hissing noise as it met the water. Sidah returned the gold to the flat stone and resumed his steady hammering. "Now the gold has been tempered and quenched, or heated and cooled, making it flexible once again."

Jomar could not keep his eyes from the process. "How can you work with metal so thin?" he asked after a time.

"I can because I must," Sidah answered sharply. "Gold is so valuable and hard to obtain that it's essential we use as little of it as possible."

Jomar stood close to Sidah, admiring his mastery and savoring the repetition of the steady beats. Two beats, then one. Two beats, then one. Was Zefa also listening to the rhythm of the hammer? *Zefa!* He must banish her from his mind.

After a while, Sidah showed Jomar that the gold was now in the form of a flat, rough circle. "How will you know when it's been hammered enough?" Jomar asked.

Sidah answered without looking up. "It's the look of it . . . the thickness . . . how even it is." He shook his head. "I simply know when to stop. If you have a talent for this, someday you'll know as well."

As Jomar listened to the sounds of the hammer blows that thinned and stretched the gold, he thought again of his old life. How had he known how deep to plant the barley seeds, how much water to give to the farm animals, how to protect the young fruit trees against the burning sun? He knew because he had watched his father do these things and more since he'd been a little boy. He smiled. For the first time he realized that Abban had learned his craft in the same slow way.

Jomar's musing came to an end at Sidah's command. "Bring that down," he said, pointing to a clay pot on the shelf. "Before the gilding, we must coat the wooden head in order to glue the gold to the wood."

The pot was full of a congealed black sludge. "This looks like the tar we use to waterproof our boats," Jomar said.

"It's the same substance. It's found in abundance in the streams around the city, and is one of the few things—besides mud, clay, and reeds—that we don't have to import," Sidah said ruefully. "Put the pot in the furnace to melt the tar, but don't let it get too hot."

The workshop filled with such a strong, acrid odor that Jomar's eyes smarted. *How strange to join costly gold with messy tar.* "Did you use this on Bittatti's jewelry?" Jomar asked.

"It wasn't necessary," Sidah said. "Tar is used only when gold goes on top of another material, such as reed or wood. For example, gold beads look simple, but they're difficult to do. Few know that inside the beads are small wooden balls first covered with tar, then with gold foil."

Again Sidah was sharing a secret with him from the mysterious world of goldsmithing.

"Has the tar softened?" Sidah asked after a while.

Jomar used the tongs to take the clay pot out of the furnace and studied the melted mass that looked like black honey. "I think it's ready."

Sidah got up and stirred the tar with a reed brush, then nodded. "Good. It's hot but not smoking." Expertly wielding the brush, he began to cover the wooden head that lay faceup on the worktable. "Watch me closely. The tar must go on smoothly to bond well with the gold."

Jomar stared as the head turned black. Now it looked even less like a bull and more like a demon with gouged pits for eyes and a double thickness of tar over its muzzle. How could this strange black blob be transformed into something splendid?

20 INTRUSIONS

The day began to darken. Sidah lit the oil lamps and worked without pause with Jomar watching by his side. "Finish the tarring while I begin the next—" Wide-eyed, he stopped speaking as a man dashed through the living area into the workshop. A man who acted as if he were being pursued.

"Qat-nu!" Jomar cried out. "Why are you here?"

"I only have a moment—Malak's on his way! Hide your sister!" The slave looked around the room with darting eyes. "Now, now! Malak is coming to get her! It will go poorly with the goldsmith if he's been hiding her. Malak must not see me. He knows I helped you escape!"

Qat-nu sprinted from the room, but not before Jomar saw that the slave's back was covered with fresh lash marks.

"Who is this man and who is Malak?" Sidah asked, his voice rising in anger. "What haven't you told me?"

Jomar's cheeks burned. "I'll explain everything as soon as Zefa's hidden!" He rushed into the cooking area, with Sidah following him. It was clear from Nari's round, staring eyes and Zefa's white face that they had seen the slave and heard his urgent warning.

Charged with desperate energy, Jomar flung open the lid of a large storage basket half-filled with barley. "Get in! Don't move!" he said to Zefa. She was so stiff with dread that he had to lift her into the basket and push her head down. He darted back to the workroom just as Malak burst in to fill the small room with his bulk and bluster.

Sidah spread out his arms to block his work area. "You don't belong here!"

"I'm a temple official in charge of irrigation crews," Malak said haughtily. "I'm not here to steal your gold, but to take back what's mine. That would be a young slave girl who escaped with her brother from my work camp."

Jomar heard Sidah's quick, astonished intake of breath. "A slave? Why do you call this boy's young sister a slave?"

"I proclaimed her to be one when I found her without her parents far from home." Malak looked at Jomar with contempt. "This boy is too young to assume the duties of a parent."

Sidah's eyes narrowed. "Why do you want this young girl returned to you?"

"She plays a lyre and sings well," Malak answered. "I want her to entertain my men after their workday is over."

"No!" Sidah shouted. "You will not have her!"

"But I will," Malak said. He walked to the three cots and threw off the blankets covering them. He went outside to search the little washroom, then stormed back and entered the workshop. "You may be an acclaimed craftsman," he said to Sidah, "but that doesn't give you the right to protect a runaway slave." He saw Zefa's bedding on the floor and kicked them to one side. "So this is where she sleeps!" Returning to the living quarters, he flung open the basket filled with lentils. Jomar held his breath—the barley basket next to it shook almost imperceptibly.

"These baskets hold grain, not young girls!" Sidah cried out.

"You've hidden her well, master goldsmith, but I'll see to it that you bear a double punishment for housing a slave and concealing her from me!"

Nari entered the workshop with a wild look in her eyes. "You say that Zefa is a runaway slave, but she's more than that. She's a thief!"

Sidah looked stunned, then his hands bunched into fists. "What right do you have to say that?" he yelled at his wife.

"The house is small. I have ears," Nari said, but fear was on her face.

Malak listened intently. "A thief as well as a runaway? What was stolen?"

"A lapis bead is missing," Nari said in a hoarse whisper.

Jomar spoke in a loud voice. "No one knows who took the bead!"

"I know you think your sister stole it," Nari said with an icy stare.

Jomar received her words like a blow. How stupid he had been to have let Nari overhear his conversation with Zefa!

Malak watched and listened with bright eyes. "We have an excellent test for determining guilt. Someone accused of a crime is thrown into the waters of our sacred river. If the suspect comes to the surface and is able to get to dry land, the river will find that person innocent. If the person drowns, the river will have judged the offender guilty. The river is low in this time of drought, so your sister will be taken to a bridge over a canal in the heart of the city."

Jomar heard Malak's words as if he were inside a nightmare. This was the same bridge they had come upon on their way to Sidah's house.

Sidah glared at Malak. "You're cruel to this young girl!"

"Am I?" Malak asked with feigned concern. "Then I have a plan that will spare her. If she becomes a permanent member of my crews, I will forget that I ever heard about the theft."

Sidah threw up his hands. "This is a terrible choice to make!"

"But it's the one I'm offering," Malak said. "To-morrow I'm ordered back to the farmlands, but I'll find out the little lyre player's decision when I return."

He left abruptly. The house seemed emptied and hushed without him.

The silence did not last long. Zefa rose out of the basket, the cover falling to the floor. "I heard what Malak said about the river test," she sobbed with tears of terror on her face. "I was close to that bridge where a man was about to be thrown into the water—I couldn't bear to look."

"I know you've wanted these children gone from this house!" Sidah shouted at Nari in a fury. "You couldn't remove Jomar, so you decided that what you overheard between Jomar and his sister would serve as a reason to be rid of Zefa." Then his voice broke. "But you've done something wrong—some-thing wicked. Would you have two young people full of life and talent lost to the waters?"

Nari did not answer her husband, but her eyes became wet and red. She made a beseeching move-ment with her hands toward her husband, which was met with a stony face. Still weeping, her hands went out to Zefa, who shook her head and walked out of the workshop.

Sidah turned to Jomar with blazing eyes. "Now tell the story you've kept from us!"

Stammering with embarrassment, Jomar spilled out the whole tale of their journey to Ur—the work crew who came upon them, Malak's enslavement of Zefa, and their escape with Qat-nu's help. Finally he told Sidah of his chance meeting with Malak near the temple.

"You've kept all this a secret!" Sidah said in a rage. "Malak's position as a temple official makes him powerful. What will happen to Zefa? What will happen to us?" His voice dropped as he sank heavily into a chair. "What am I to do?"

"I'm the one who must do something," Jomar said without an idea in his head.

21 JOMAR'S PLEA

The stricken expressions of the goldsmith and his wife did not change after hearing Jomar's brave promise of action. He didn't blame them. What could he do? Somehow he must find Zefa a safe place to live beyond Malak's reach. And Sidah must be freed from the charge of housing and concealing a runaway slave. *Impossible!*

Jomar needed to be alone. "May I have your permission to go out for a short while?" he asked Sidah, who waved his consent without looking up.

Jomar moved restlessly through the neighborhood. Everything around him was the color of mud, so he was only dimly aware of the dusty roads he walked upon or the small brick dwellings he passed. But he scanned the streets constantly for Malak, his heart racing at a glimpse of every tall man, every stout man, every bald man.

How could he do battle with Malak, a temple official? He had nowhere to turn; he knew no one more powerful. Jomar came to a sudden halt. He did know someone more powerful. *The high priestess Bittatti!* He would go to her and plead for help. He knew that Sidah would never give him permission to do so. He would go without his permission.

Jomar hurried to the temple and flung open the rear entrance door. His heart sank. An unfamiliar guard was on duty, not the friendly man who had first admitted him.

"Not so fast," the guard said, blocking Jomar's approach. "This entrance is restricted to officials and craftsmen. Who are you?"

Jomar tried to act calm and trustworthy. "I'm the new apprentice to the goldsmith Sidah."

The guard's eyes were tight with suspicion. "Maybe you are, maybe you aren't. Show me some proof."

Jomar could think of nothing clever to say to prove his relationship to Sidah. "I've—I've forgotten the goldsmith's cylinder seal," he said haltingly. Without a word the guard grabbed his arm and roughly escorted him out of the building.

Jomar considered returning to the workshop to take the seal when Sidah wasn't looking. But if Sidah found it missing, he would think that both he and Zefa were thieves.

Entering the back door of the temple hadn't worked. He'd try the front door. Running around the huge building and mounting the stairs two at a time, he entered the temple through the mighty cedar doors. When he saw a guard looking at him, Jomar tried to conceal his labored breathing. He began to walk in an assured manner, as if he had every right to be in the temple.

Drawn by the smell of sweet burning incense, Jomar came upon a bearded statue of the moongod Nanna lit by hundreds of flickering candles. In front of the powerful image, a long, waist-high table was heaped with offerings of fruit and grain. *My family could have lived on this food for a month,* Jomar thought bitterly. He shook his head—he must concentrate on the task before him.

As Jomar neared the chambers of the high priestess, he was surprised to find no handmaiden at her door. Hearing voices nearby, he looked around a corner and saw the young woman and a guard talking and laughing together. He ducked back. They were distracted by their interest in each other. This was his chance!

Jomar raised his hand to knock on Bittatti's door, then lowered it. He must get inside quietly or the noise of his knocking might bring both the hand-maiden and the guard to the chambers. Although it took more courage than Jomar thought he possessed, he opened the door and slipped into the room. He straightened his shoulders. He must be direct and dignified.

The high priestess was seated on her chair as if she hadn't moved from their first meeting. Her elegant golden headdress and earrings gleamed as before. But when she saw Jomar, Bittatti flinched with alarm and put a hand to her throat. Recognizing Jomar, her hand dropped and her face stiffened. "Ah, it's the goldsmith's new apprentice who enters my chambers unannounced," she said in a harsh tone. "Is this what Sidah would want you to be doing?"

"No!" Jomar said. "He knows nothing of this."

"I've been waiting for my new necklace for a long time," Bittatti said with narrowed eyes. "Perhaps you're delivering it to me at last."

"Yes—I mean no!" Jomar blurted, then tried to collect himself. "Sidah wants to present the necklace to you himself."

"You've entered my chamber without permission. You don't have my necklace." Bittatti's voice was as cold as her eyes. "Why are you here?"

Jomar's attempt to remain dignified failed. He sank to the floor and held up his open hands to her. "I come to beg for your help. Both Sidah and my young sister are in danger. May I have your permission to tell you what's happened to them?"

The high priestess looked down on Jomar as she spoke. "Nothing must interfere with the goldsmith's work. It was I who told the music director he must insist that Sidah embellish the great lyre in time for the new year celebration. I want all who come here for the ceremonies to behold how mighty the moongod's temple is to have a craftsman able to create such a lyre. Sidah must be protected, so I will listen to your story." She motioned Jomar to stand with a flick of her finger. "Be brief."

Jomar took a deep breath. He told the high priestess about Malak coming upon them when his sister was playing her lyre and singing her song to the moongod. He told her of Malak's enslavement of Zefa and his plan of keeping her with him in order to have his workers entertained when their workday was over.

"Entertained?" Bittatti said with arched eyebrows. "I know of this man Malak. When one of my handmaidens was poorly used by him, I had him demoted in rank and sent out of the city to manage irrigation crews."

Unsure how to respond to this information, Jomar rushed on. He told Bittatti about their escape from the work crew and their arrival in Ur. He told her of Malak's angry visit to the goldsmith's house and his threat to punish Sidah for housing and hiding a runaway slave. He did not tell the high priestess of the missing lapis bead or the coming river ordeal.

"The charge against Sidah is serious," Bittatti said. "What is his relationship to your sister?"

"Sidah has heard her play and sing," Jomar answered. "He feels Zefa was sent by the gods to inspire his work on the great temple lyre."

"Sent by the gods?" Bittatti said. "It's hard for me to believe that an untrained country girl is so skilled a musician."

"Sidah believes she has a great natural talent." Jomar turned away from Bittatti's harsh gaze when he felt his face redden. "Until recently I have paid little attention to her music making."

"Brothers frequently ignore their young sisters and often know nothing of their worth," the high priestess said bitingly. "I've given you enough of my time. How will Sidah be saved?"

Jomar was surprised by her question, but found he had the seeds of an answer in his head. "The gatekeeper at the entrance to the city spoke of temple musicians. If my sister could be—"

Bittatti interrupted him. "I have listened to you out of concern for Sidah. Now you will wait until I decide what is to be done." She held up her palm to indicate that the interview was over, then briskly clapped her hands together. Her frightened hand-maiden entered the room. "You were not guarding my door when this brash young man entered my chambers unannounced."

The handmaiden prostrated herself in front of the high priestess, her arms stretched out in front of her. "I beg forgiveness. My place is outside your chambers. I will not abandon my responsibilities again."

When Bittatti nodded briefly, the young woman rose and slowly walked backward toward the door in order to leave the room while facing the high priestess.

In a similar state of awe, Jomar did the same.

22 SO MANY STEPS

Frightened about telling Sidah where he'd been, Jomar walked slowly back to the goldsmith's house. It was almost dark when he returned. He found Gamil outside his house, throwing his ball high in the air and catching it with one hand as it fell.

In spite of his turmoil, Jomar made himself be friendly. "How's your mother?"

"Her pain is worse in the early morning," Gamil said, then fell silent as he absently passed his ball from hand to hand. "If you have time, I'd like to speak with you for a moment about what goes on in the goldsmith's workshop," he finally said.

Jomar was instantly uneasy. "I've a message I must deliver to Sidah. Perhaps tomorrow." Gamil's face fell with disappointment.

The goldsmith and his wife were sitting glumly at the table, their uneaten meal in front of them.

Zefa wasn't there. Probably Nari had sent her out on some errand.

"Where have you been?" Sidah asked his apprentice in a tight voice.

Jomar took several deep breaths. He had kept too many secrets from Sidah. "I went to the high priestess and told her of our difficulties with Malak."

Sidah's eyes glared with anger. "You went to that exalted woman with our problems? And she listened to you? Had you asked me, as you should have, I would never have given you permission to do such a thing." Sidah's tone became less harsh. "You've done something few people would be brave enough, or foolish enough, to do. What did she say to you?"

"She told me she instructed the music director to insist that you embellish the lyre in time for the new year ceremony," Jomar said.

Sidah's eyes were wide with surprise. "She told you that? That explains Kurgal's uncharacteristic behavior. What else did she tell you?"

"She will consider your situation because she wants no harm to come to you that could interfere with the completion of the lyre's embellishment," Jomar said.

"Your news is hopeful. Mine is not," Sidah said. "Your sister has disappeared. She slipped away just after Malak's visit, taking her basket with her. Nari searched for her a long time without success."

Thoughts of the high priestess flew out of his head. "Zefa gone? I'll go look for her! How will she find food? Where will she sleep?"

Sidah shook his head. "It's too dark to search for her now, but go tomorrow just before dawn. But you must be in the workroom at sunrise."

Jomar forced himself to eat dinner, then went to his cot to lie there, tense with worry. When he finally fell asleep, he dreamt of Zefa struggling in the canal, her long hair streaming out and slowly turning the swirling water black.

He awoke before dawn the next morning to find his blankets tangled together and his body half-off the cot. He quickly got out of bed and left the house. Should he call out Zefa's name? He would only wake those sleeping in the small mud-brick houses that hugged the street. Jomar hurried through one quiet neighborhood after another, all free of the noise and dust that would be everywhere when the city awoke. He stopped at every place that could attract or conceal a young, slight girl, but found only a mangy dog who begged for food and friendship. Jomar patted its head and ran a hand over its thin body, but moved on. He looked for Zefa until the dawn broke, but then he had to honor Sidah's instructions and return without her.

Sidah's bed was empty. When Jomar entered the workroom, he saw that the cotton shroud had been removed from the lyre.

"I can see you've been unsuccessful—but you'll try again," Sidah said. "Time is running out, Jomar. Yesterday we lost a full afternoon of work. Heat the tar and finish coating the head while I return to hammering the gold."

In comparison with the rough coating that had covered the marsh boats, the tar that Sidah had applied to the head already seemed smooth and evenly distributed. But Jomar was filled with a painful memory. Once, failing to tar his reed boat carefully, it had sprung a leak in the middle of a marsh lake, slowly sinking beneath the surface and taking Jomar with it. After wild and exhausting thrashing in the water, he had managed to make his way back to the shore. He would make his tarring as perfect as he could.

Imitating the way Sidah grasped the brush, Jomar dipped it repeatedly into the black, gummy liquid to make long, smooth strokes over the bull's blackened head. He was so intent on his work that he failed to notice that the hammering had stopped. Sidah was at his side with a sheet of gold in his hands almost as thin as the leaves in Bittatti's necklace. Jomar stepped away from the table as Sidah deftly laid the gold over the head. Then with quick, sure chisel strokes, he removed the gold from the places where the eyes, ears, horns, and forelock would go, and returned the excess to the flat stone.

Jomar had expected a wondrous transformation when the gold covered the tar, but the head remained ill-formed and strange. "Why did you put on the gold, then take some off?"

"I've told you—gold is so costly that we must

use it sparingly," Sidah answered. He pointed to a basket on the shelf. "Bring that down."

Jomar found the ears and horns nestled against one another in the basket. All four pieces had pegs of wood attached to their bases. The long, graceful horns had sharp tips of lapis. Jomar thought of the splendid living bull that he had seen at the temple's new year ceremony so long ago. "I remember seeing a bull about to be sacrificed with tips of gold on its horns. Why are these tipped with—" he started to ask.

"With lapis?" Sidah broke in. "When the head is finished, the effect will be striking. I'm going to cover a horn with tar. Watch how I do it, because you'll do the second one. Notice that I don't touch the lapis tips with the tar."

What Sidah was asking him to do seemed impossible. "Even after watching you, I don't think I'll be able to do this," Jomar said. Under his breath he muttered, "I'm not your son."

"I know," Sidah snapped. "But you're here and he's not."

Startled by the force of Sidah's answer, Jomar focused on watching Sidah tar the horn. Then it was his turn. It was not a simple task to brush the black, honey-like material over the horn's cylindrical surface. He worked slowly, while Sidah returned to working on the head. While he was applying the tar, Jomar glanced at the bull's golden head. Again he had expected a wonderful transformation, but this was not the case. It still didn't look like a bull, and it lacked the luster of Bittatti's gleaming jewelry. "How will you make the gold shine?"

"With slow, careful work," Sidah answered. "First the bull must be given a lifelike muzzle. His eyes must be strong and challenging. The head must be made ready to receive the ears and horns. Finally, the piece must be polished to bring out the luster you admire."

So many steps, Jomar said to himself.

Sidah looked at Jomar as if he could read his thoughts. "There are many tasks ahead of us. In a way it's not unlike the slow, careful work of planting and harvesting."

"But working with gold is much more difficult," Jomar said.

"That's because farm work seems natural to

you," Sidah said. "But I know it must have taken your father years to acquire his knowledge of plants and animals, weather and soil."

Jomar mulled over what Sidah had said. "I think you're right, but why did you choose a farm boy who knew nothing about gold to be your apprentice?"

Sidah paused before answering. "I had just lost Abban when I met your father. I was moved when he told me how much he would miss your skills and energy after you left the farm." Sidah's eyes misted. "He said he would miss your company most of all."

"My father said that? I didn't know he felt that way about me."

Sidah seemed to struggle with himself before speaking. "I'm glad I told you," he finally said. "I made the same mistake with Abban. I told him how proud I was of his skills, but not that I loved him as a person, as a companion."

Jomar looked down and saw his father's sandals on his feet. And was ashamed. He'd been so angry at being sent to Ur and having to be reponsible for Zefa that he had neglected to thank his father for giving him his own sandals and accepting his frayed ones in return.

Jomar decided to ask Sidah a question that had bothered him for a long time. "When you made an agreement with my father to accept me as your apprentice, you didn't think I'd be helping you with the lyre, did you?"

Sidah stopped working, his hands idle in his lap. "You're right—I wouldn't have chosen you if I'd known. When your father and I talked, I thought you would be helping me with my usual assignments—making jewelry, drinking straws, ceremonial weapons."

"Even though you made an agreement with my father, I don't think Nari wants me here," Jomar said quietly.

"Nari was hurt and angry when I told her I'd accepted you as my apprentice so soon after Abban's death," Sidah said. "It was my right to make such an arrangement, but I should have given her more time to mourn. He was her son as well as mine." Sidah shook his head sadly as if to rid it of these thoughts.

He returned to his work, now pressing the gold sheet against the tarred wooden bull's head with a hammer covered with leather. Again Jomar was lulled by the refrain of Sidah's steady rhythm.

23 NARI'S WISH

Nari came quietly into the workroom bringing the midday meal. After setting it down she held her hands tightly together in front of her chest.

"The bull begins to take shape," she said softly.

Sidah nodded. "It goes forward at a steady pace. And I have an apprentice who asks many questions." He paused. "Good questions."

Nari looked directly at Sidah. "Your answers are good as well."

Sidah stopped hammering. "I'm glad you overheard them," he finally said.

"I must say something to you," Nari said, glancing nervously at Jomar before speaking to her husband in a trembly voice. "We've not given our son the ceremonial rites the dead deserve."

Sidah stared at his wife. "How could we, Nari? Abban's body was never recovered from the waters."

She seemed not to hear him. "I know Abban is unhappy because he wasn't properly buried in the vault beneath our floor, nor has he been offered food and drink to sustain him." She kneaded her hands together, and her eyes filled with tears. "I have a request to make."

"And what is that?" Sidah asked.

Nari spoke rapidly, a look of raw hope and longing on her face. "After you have completed your work on the lyre, I'd like to have a proper funeral ceremony for Abban. My hope is that Zefa will return and create a praise song for our son and accompany her song on the temple lyre."

"Zefa? Who is now in danger because you told Malak about the missing bead?" Sidah asked with astonishment.

"I will never forgive myself for telling Malak about the theft," Nari said with quiet urgency. "But as I listened to her play and sing for you, I found her music more important than the lapis bead. I think her song could give our son the serenity he seeks."

Sidah's face melted. "I know you search for peace

as well. If Zefa is found, we'll ask her if she is willing to do what you wish."

As he listened to Nari, Jomar churned with reactions that warred with each other. He was surprised by her request. He was moved by her apology. At the same time, how could she ask Zefa, whose life Nari had thrown into terrible danger, to do something as important as singing for her dead son?

As if she knew his thoughts, Nari looked beseechingly at Jomar. She started to speak, but then turned and left the workroom with her hands still clasped in front of her. Her expression of need and vulnerability was one that Jomar had never seen before.

24 THE LYRE STANDS WATCH

"My wife asks a great deal of Zefa," Sidah said. "Even if she's found and returns to us, I can't believe she'll do what Nari wants."

"I'm not sure what she'll decide to do," Jomar said, cutting the conversation short. He knew he must put Zefa out of his mind and concentrate on his tasks. He finished tarring the second horn and brought it to Sidah. A grunt told him his work had been accepted.

"And now the ears must be tarred," Sidah said.

Jomar sighed. "They look harder to do than the horns."

"Perhaps, but your fingers will remember what they learned from working on the horn," Sidah said. Jomar wasn't sure what this meant, but he stood next to Sidah as the goldsmith slowly blackened the turns and folds of the ear.

When it was his turn to tar the second ear, Jomar tried to recall every move that Sidah had made. He was so engrossed in what he was doing that time seemed to stop. When Sidah suddenly stood beside him, Jomar's breathing quickened and his hands began to tremble.

"You were correct in thinking that the ears are more difficult to do than the horns, but the tar is smooth—you've applied it evenly," Sidah finally said after closely examining his work.

Jomar breathed normally again.

"Watch as I cover a horn with gold," Sidah said. He hammered the gold on the stone, then took up a piece just large enough to cover the horn. He made a smooth transition between the gold and the lapis tip. "Now hammer the gold onto the horn, Jomar. Remember, I must handle the overlap. Work as quickly as you can so the tar retains its heat."

Trying to imitate Sidah's rhythmic beat, Jomar began to pound the gold against the tarry surface of the second horn. He hoped the goldsmith's mastery would somehow seep into his eyes, his fingers. He spent a long time working on the horn before taking it to Sidah. It was neither perfect nor a failure. Taking the mallet from Jomar's hand, Sidah made additional blows against the gold surface, then held it out for Jomar to see the corrections. "Didn't I tell you that gold is forgiving? In the places I repaired, the work was either too rough, or the gold wasn't tight enough against the tar." Again Sidah delicately made a smooth seam between the gold and lapis. After another careful inspection of the horn, he said, "Your work is satisfactory for a beginner."

"You've been testing my skills by giving me more difficult tasks than I thought you would," Jomar said.

"I had to—we have a deadline to meet. But given enough time, skills can be taught by a good teacher. I've been testing you for more than skills."

Jomar's stomach tightened. "For what then?"

Sidah gazed searchingly at Jomar. "I've been trying to decide if you have the qualities that working with gold requires."

"What qualities?" Jomar asked softly.

"Persistence, dexterity, and the ability to make the right motions in the right order," Sidah said. "And the most important thing: you must have a passion for the process of working with gold, not just for the gold itself."

Jomar was unsure that he had these qualities. He looked away from Sidah's unblinking eyes.

When the workroom began to darken, Sidah lit the lamps, and the smell of sesame oil filled Jomar's mind with images of his mother. "We must gild both ears while the tar is still warm enough to hold the gold. I'll do one, you will do the other."

But this was the time that Jomar thought he would be out looking for Zefa! Comforted only by the familiar scent of the oil, Jomar bent over the workbench to gild one of the ears. He showed his work to Sidah when he thought the job was done. The goldsmith held the ears next to each other to point out differences between the two. After making some corrections to Jomar's ear, Sidah again compared the ears and grunted his approval.

Jomar thought of Abban, experienced and gifted. For his own work Sidah's grunt would have to do.

Sidah carefully put the gilded horns and ears on a worktable. "They'll be attached when the head is ready to receive them. The night comes on and the tar has lost its heat." He threw the white cotton shroud over the lyre.

Jomar began putting the tools back on their hooks, then took up the reed broom and swept the room clean. "Why do you uncover the lyre in the morning and cover it in the evening?" he asked. "The instrument hasn't been touched since we started work on the bull's head."

"I've never thought about why I do this," Sidah answered. "I suppose it's my way of saying that the workday begins when the lyre stands watch over our labors. When it withdraws under its cotton blanket, we also rest."

Jomar nodded and banked the coals. "What about the strong, staring eyes you promised?"

"Tomorrow," Sidah answered with a tired smile. "We've had a full day, so you don't have much time to search for Zefa. Go out and look for her before darkness comes."

25 ANOTHER PAIR OF EYES

Jomar walked out to find the shadowy streets almost deserted. He stopped every person he saw to describe his sister and ask if she'd been seen. All shook their heads and hurried on. Jomar felt a pull on his heart. *They're all going home, but Zefa has no home.*

A kind-faced man returning to his house with a cart stacked with unsold woven textiles listened sympathetically. "This city is full of wandering children without parents, all with black hair and eyes," he said. "In times of famine the temple priests often buy the sons and daughters of farm families who are unable to feed them. But if they're found to be unsuitable for temple work, they're turned out onto the streets."

"Turned out?" Jomar asked. "How can the children survive?"

The man shook his head sadly. "I see children in

the early morning picking over whatever garbage they can find before scurrying away like vermin."

Garbage dumps. Why hadn't he thought of this? He nodded his thanks to the man, then began to look for Zefa near every mound of rotting food. Repeatedly calling out her name disturbed the rats feeding on the reeking waste, but brought no answer from Zefa. Finally it was utter darkness and discouragement that brought him home.

Jomar's body held so much fear that the meal Nari had left for him went uneaten. Falling into an exhausted sleep, he dreamed of the abandoned dog who had pleaded for food and protection. *Was Zefa doing the same thing?*

Jomar was up before dawn the next day to continue his search for Zefa. As he passed Gamil's house, he heard a woman's soft, insistent moaning. From another house came a baby's wail and the shushing sounds of its mother. The air still held the slightly rancid smell of oil in which fish had been cooked the day before. He methodically went up one street and down another, going farther and farther away from the temple. Now alert to the presence of children at this hour, Jomar strained to see them in the half light of the morning.

Two thinly dressed boys were going through a small garbage dump. Jomar went up to them and asked what would be a good place to look for a young homeless girl.

"Some of us crowd around a bonfire behind the temple," the older boy answered. "It helps us bear the cold, but we need food more than warmth." The boys returned to their hunt for edible scraps. Jomar remembered well the painful cramp of hunger, and wished them luck in their search. He found a handful of children at the back of the temple huddled around a little fire, their hands stretched out to receive the heat. Zefa was not among them. He returned home to find Nari and Sidah still asleep. He lay on his cot, heartsick and exhausted, and slept.

Later that morning, Nari served him a bowl of honey-flavored mush. He wanted to take it to the children, but Sidah was waiting for him. He gulped down the meal, managed a small smile of thanks to

Nari, then hurried to the workroom. The lyre was without its cotton covering and the pungent oil lamps were again burning in the shadowy room.

Sidah was hunched over a worktable running his fingers lovingly over two eyes made of lapis and shell. He darted a look at Jomar. "I'm sorry. The city can easily swallow up a small girl." He returned to his task. "These wonderful eyes were made by craftsmen at the temple. Of course, shells are not as rare or costly as gold or lapis, but shells make beautiful inlays if used skillfully."

Jomar made an effort to stop thinking about Zefa and rejoin Sidah's world. "I saw them worked into a design on the back of Bittatti's chair."

"Ah, you noticed. When the head is finished, the bull's gaze must be forceful."

"Should I heat the tar?" Jomar asked, hoping that Sidah did not have another assignment that would prevent him from seeing him insert the eyes.

Sidah nodded. "Yes, heat the tar, then fill in the two hollows in the wooden head with it. The eyes interest you, so stand close and watch me attach them to the head." When the hot tar was in position,

Sidah carefully placed the lapis-and-shell eyes on the sides of the head. It was slow work to make the eyes match each other perfectly.

Jomar stared. They were like Bittatti's heavily outlined eyes, dramatic and piercing. "I can't wait for all the pieces to come together," he breathed.

"Ah, but you must," Sidah said. "Like the flowering of a date palm, it will happen in its own order and at its own pace." He took up a flat tool, and slowly began to transform the crude, bulbous muzzle into two flaring nostrils over thin, down-turned lips. Then he pressed crisp lines around the bull's nose and mouth with a sharp chasing tool.

Jomar saw the head becoming more alive. "That looks exactly like the nose and mouth of a real bull!"

Sidah nodded. "I know the look of cattle. I grew up on a farm."

"You did?" Jomar asked with surprise.

"I left when I was a young man to become an apprentice to a traveling coppersmith," Sidah said. "We went from village to village to make farm tools and repair old ones."

"When I was a little boy, my father would take

me to our village when the coppersmith visited," Jomar said. "I watched the man pour melted copper into molds. When the liquid hardened into a tool, I thought he must be a magician. How did you become a goldsmith?"

"I met Nari in one of the villages I visited," Sidah answered, his voice turning tender. "She was lively—full of laughter. Her father died shortly after he had given us permission to wed, so we were free to come here to live after our marriage. I already knew how to work with metal, so a temple gold-smith chose me over others to be his apprentice."

"I thought all apprentices were young," Jomar said. "You were already a man."

Sidah's face darkened. "I was a man, a copper-smith, a father, but I was treated as if I were an ignorant farm boy."

Like me! "Why did you stay with the goldsmith?"

"I had some talent for working with metal, and this was my opportunity to learn a difficult craft," Sidah said. "After he died, the temple asked me to take his place."

While Jomar watched, Sidah worked quietly on

the muzzle for a long while. "While you were look-ing for Zefa last evening, I joined my friends and heard good news," he finally said. "The snow in the northern mountains has begun to melt. The river will become mighty once again, and the canals and reservoirs will receive its waters."

Jomar's spirits rose. "My father must be clearing away dead roots to prepare the fields for planting!"

"And you might be longing to return to the life you know, with or without Zefa," Sidah said. "Even though your father and I made an agreement, I wouldn't insist that you stay here if your heart is elsewhere." Sidah threw the shroud over the lyre with a decisive gesture. "Give me your answer when work on the lyre is completed."

Jomar was bewildered. Was Sidah offering him the opportunity to return home out of compassion? Or was this a kind way of letting Jomar know that he lacked the qualities necessary to become a fine goldsmith? He could no longer make Sidah or his father responsible for his future. The decision to stay or go was his.

In the evening Jomar went out to search for Zefa

in neighborhoods farther from the temple and new to him, but the little mud-brick houses, clustered together as if for comfort and warmth, looked the same. He walked the streets calling her name, looking for her, listening for her. As day disappeared into night, the homes brightened, one by one, when oil lamps were lit. He could hear the hum of conversations inside the houses. The most distinct voices were those of children shouting, playing games, and laughing. He had lived with Zefa for so many years. Why couldn't he remember doing these things with her?

26 SOMETHING MORE IS NEEDED

Sidah and Nari were asleep when he returned. Jomar's supper was waiting for him, but he was too miserable to do anything but pick at his food. He lay down on his cot yearning for sleep free of nightmares.

He woke just before dawn with his mind filled with a pattern of recurring notes. Two beats, then a pause; two beats, a pause. Why was this familiar to him? Was it the cadence of Sidah's steady hammering? Jomar sat bolt upright. No, it was the rhythm of the song that the little band of street children had played for Zefa when they first entered the city. He would go back to the bazaar when crowds of people roaming through the area would provide an audience for the band. If his hunch was correct, he would find Zefa. The band was without a lyre player!

Too excited to sleep, Jomar got up and tiptoed to the workshop. He wandered about the room, peering closely at everything in the murky light. He touched all of the tools and named them under his breath. Clinging to the side of the flat stone was a bit of gold he hadn't noticed before. The gilded bull's head lay on the worktable waiting to be brought to life by Sidah, whose penetrating gaze could go beneath the gold, the tar, the wood to the spirit of the bull itself.

The sun was slanting into the room from the high windows when Sidah joined him. "You and the sungod were up before me," he said, sliding the lyre's shroud to the floor. "Why aren't you out looking for Zefa?"

"She might have returned to the bazaar near the entrance to the city," Jomar said. "May I have your permission to search for her while you're having your midday meal?"

Sidah hesitated before answering. "You seem confident of finding her. Yes, go out at noon, but we must work hard this morning. No distractions."

"No distractions," Jomar repeated.

"The tar must be hot to attach the ears and horns," Sidah said. "The golden head must be polished; a slow, tedious process." From a shelf he got down a pot of fine-powdered limestone and a smooth stone the size of a small egg. Sidah demonstrated what Jomar was to do by sprinkling the abrasive powder over one of the ears, then rubbing it for a moment with the little stone. "Polish the ears and horns while I finish securing the gold to the head."

The sharp smell of heating tar pervaded the workshop, but Jomar was no longer bothered by the odor. He worked steadily on the ears and horns with the burnishing stone all through the morning. Because the pieces became smoother and more lustrous with every stroke, Jomar worked without feeling the tedium that Sidah had predicted.

Nari came in and stood looking at the bull's head. "Soon your work on the lyre will be finished," she murmured before returning to the kitchen.

Jomar knew she was thinking of the ceremony for her son, which made him think of Zefa. The missing bead. Malak. And the river test. He shook himself—he could not let these troubles interfere with his work.

"Get down an awl and watch how I attach the ear," Sidah said. Without having to think Jomar handed him the sharp, pointed tool. With it Sidah made two holes on each side of the head. Removing the pot of tar from the furnace, he dipped the wooden peg attached to the ear into the tar. After carefully pushing the peg through one of the holes, he adjusted the position of the ear so that it stood out sharply from the side of the head.

"That's exactly the right angle for an alert bull ready for anything!" Jomar said.

Sidah suppressed a small smile. "Attach the second ear."

Following Sidah's example Jomar tarred the peg and pushed it through the hole, then tried to position the ear so that it mirrored Sidah's ear perfectly. He looked up questioningly when he thought he had succeeded. Sidah made a grunting noise deep in his throat.

"And now the horns?" Jomar asked.

"And now the horns," Sidah said. "I'll do the first one, you will do the second."

Jomar watched closely as Sidah went through the slow process of gluing one of the horns to the head with tar. When it was his turn, Jomar repeated what Sidah had done. After countless small adjustments, he stood back from the table and saw that both horns rose from the head with the same graceful, thrusting angle. Again he nervously waited for Sidah's response to his work.

Sidah nodded, but his mind seemed elsewhere. "The bull is stately, but it's not finished. Something more is needed. Do you know what that might be?"

Jomar wondered what more could possibly be added to the bull's head. Then he knew what was missing. The head should be more than a faithful likeness of the animal, more than a splendid decoration for the lyre. The bull should look like a god.

"A beard," Jomar said. "The statue of the moon-god in the temple has a beard, and it makes Nanna look grand and powerful."

Sidah looked startled, then was quiet for a moment. "We've come to a good stopping place. Go and search for Zefa. I'll go to the temple to give Bittatti her necklace and thank her for listening to your story. When I come home, I'll have something wonderful to show you, something that's been waiting for me at the treasury for a long time."

27 IN THE BAZAAR

Although they would soon go their separate ways, Sidah and Jomar left the house together. They found Gamil leaning against the brick wall of his house next door. Jomar was struck by his somber expression. "I was saddened to hear your mother cry out in the early morning yesterday," Jomar said to him.

"Yes, it was a difficult time for her," Gamil replied. He turned to Sidah and spoke in a soft voice. "My mother misses your wife's daily visits."

Sidah looked pained. "I know how ill your mother is, but I told Nari she's not to go to your home anymore. You were Abban's closest friend, but you haven't been to our house to offer your sympathies since his death." Sidah abruptly swung away to begin his walk to the temple. Gamil entered his house with a stricken look on his face.

Jomar pondered their brief conversation as he

started off to find Zefa. He didn't know why Gamil
had avoided Sidah, but it was clear they both felt hurt
and abandoned. But he must stop thinking about
their problems—his mission was to find his sister.

After a few false turns, Jomar found himself back
in the bustling bazaar that had astonished him when
he first entered the city. As before, he moved among
merchants, housewives, slaves, and vendors. Ignoring
the smell of roasted mutton, and looking away from
the tempting goods laid out for sale, he concentrat-
ed on listening for the music of the beggar band.

Jomar walked through the crowded marketplace
twice without hearing it. Then—the faint sound of
that tinny music! He strained to hear the notes of a
lyre, but it was only when he came close that he
spotted Zefa. He concealed himself behind several
listeners so he could look at her for a moment
unobserved. She was thin and her tunic was worn
and dirty, but she sang and played with energy. Like
the other raggedy children, her eyes searched the
audience for approval or sympathy.

A handful of people stood listening with him.
At the end of the song, the boy with the tambourine

placed it on the ground. He made a beseeching gesture with his hands, then brought them to his
mouth. A man placed an uneaten piece of broiled
rabbit on the tambourine. A woman bent to add
grapes and a few plums. When the others drifted
away, Zefa saw Jomar.

"I've been looking everywhere for you," Jomar said
quietly, noticing that she was making an effort to
conceal her surprise.

"Well, now you've found me."

The children in the little band stood listening,
their darting eyes reflecting their interest in the conversation. Jomar moved closer to avoid being overheard. "You might have come to me before leaving."

Zefa moved back a step. "Why would I do such
a thing? Even before we left home you let me know
I was a burden to you."

Jomar was stung by her comment, but ignored it.
"I would have liked to have been a part of your decision," he said in a voice he hoped sounded confident.

Zefa shook her head. "You would have tried to
prevent me from leaving. You're lucky I left, because
now you're no longer responsible for me. I overheard

Sidah say you'd have to give up your apprenticeship if you couldn't find a job for me. And if I did go back, Malak would find me, and my problems would only get worse."

Jomar felt his gut tighten. Without thinking he held out his hand to her. "They're our problems— we must stay together."

Zefa rejected his hand, but her voice lost its edge. She pointed to the little band of players nearby. "My friends are waiting for me."

"Your friends?"

"Yes, my friends," Zefa said. "We must perform in order to eat. We see that the food we receive is evenly divided. We huddle together at night to keep warm." She stared at him. "We take care of each other."

When had Zefa developed such quiet assurance? She no longer seemed frightened or in need of his protection. Jomar began to realize he could not convince her to return with him. "All right, stay if you must. But before we separate I must tell you what's happened since you left." He took her arm, and together they walked some distance away from the little band. "After Malak's visit, I went to the high priestess at the temple to plead for her help. I told her of your enslavement by Malak and Sidah's risk of punishment for concealing a runaway slave."

"Did you also tell her about the missing bead and Malak's order that I take the river test?" she asked defiantly.

"She never would have listened to me if I had," Jomar said. "But I did tell her about Sidah's respect for your musical skills and what a serious threat Malak is to you both."

Zefa's stubborn expression faded. "What did she say?"

"Only that she will decide what's to be done." Jomar lightly touched her shoulder. He continued tentatively. "There's more. Nari feels her son is unhappy because he was never given a proper funeral ceremony." Jomar paused slightly, then went on. "She wants you to return to sing a praise song for Abban and play on the temple lyre before it leaves the workshop."

Zefa's head moved backward in surprise. "*Nari* wants this?"

"She does," Jomar said. "I saw her crying when she was listening to you play on the lyre and sing for

Sidah. She believes that with your help, her son's spirit will find peace."

"Nari hasn't brought peace to mine!" Zefa said fiercely, her anger rising once again. "I suppose *you* want me to do this, don't you?"

"No, Zefa. This is for you to decide. I'll support any decision you make."

For a moment Zefa neither moved nor spoke as she reflected on what her brother had told her. Then her expression slowly changed from anger to quiet resolution. "The son she loved is dead. Maybe my song can ease her grief."

Jomar was stunned by her compassion. Filled with admiration for his sister, Jomar's attempt to be reasonable vanished, and his fears for her broke through in a rush of concern. "If Malak finds you, you can't take the river test! You don't even know how to swim!"

Zefa's black eyes snapped. "Would you rather have me be a part of Malak's work crews?"

"Never!"

Zefa spoke slowly. "Malak thought I'd be so frightened of the ordeal that I'd choose to go with him instead." She raised her chin. "But if he finds me, I'll take the test. The sacred river will judge me fairly because I'm innocent."

Jomar stared at Zefa, then his body slumped with relief. She believes in the wisdom of the river. Her willingness to take the river test could only mean one thing. "Zefa, you didn't steal the bead!"

Zefa looked at him with a steady gaze. "Of course I didn't. Why did you think I had?"

"Because you spent the night in the workshop. Because you admired some lapis beads in the bazaar. Because—"

Zefa interrupted him. "Because you didn't believe me. Go back to Sidah's. Come and get me just before the ceremony."

28 FROM THE TREASURY

Jomar had found Zefa, but he came away from her choked with emotion. When he entered the workshop, Sidah was looking down at a large package with such concentration that for a moment he seemed unaware of Jomar's presence. Then he looked up sharply. "Did you find her?"

Jomar nodded. "She's become a member of a little band of musicians that performs in the bazaar just inside the city walls."

Sidah looked around Jomar with bewilderment. "Where is she? Isn't she coming back to us?"

"She's too frightened of Malak finding her here."

"Her fears are real," Sidah said. "I must tell Nari that we'll be unable to give Abban the ceremony she wants for him."

"Wait. When the time comes, I'm to go and get

her," Jomar said. "Zefa has agreed to return to sing and play at the ceremony."

Sidah looked with wonderment at Jomar. "She had every reason to refuse. Your sister has a generous heart."

"Yes, she's generous—and more," Jomar said. "If Malak finds her, she will undergo the river ordeal because she believes only guilty people fail the test. Like you, she accepts the judgment of the river. And because she does, I know she didn't take the lapis bead."

"She didn't take the bead?" Sidah stopped speaking, so lost in thought and confusion that Jomar finally pointed to the package on the table.

"Is this what you brought back from the treasury?"

As if grateful for the distraction, Sidah eagerly took off the wrapping. He held up a beard of lapis almost as large as the bull's head and placed it underneath the bull's muzzle. He looked expectantly at Jomar. "Is this the kind of beard you had in mind?"

"This is more wonderful than anything I imagined!" Jomar said.

Sidah smiled. "I wanted to surprise you with

this, but you surprised me by recognizing that the bull should be bearded."

"But I didn't expect the beard to be of lapis," Jomar said. "You told me how fine the blue gem looks with gold, but also how rare and costly it is." He bent down to peer into the basket. "What's this smaller lapis piece?"

"The bull's forelock," Sidah answered.

Jomar looked closely at the beard and forelock. "Each of these pieces has been etched with wavy lines to look like hair! Who made them?"

"Abban and I spent days working on the design for the lyre. I received permission from the music director to give drawings and precise instructions to a temple craftsman who works only with gems. He gave me the two eyes some time ago, but it took him much longer to carve and assemble the large and intricate beard and forelock." He turned over the beard. "Both are mounted on silver." Sidah ran his hand over the pieces lovingly, then examined every detail of their complicated construction. "Heat up the tar," he finally said. "This will be the last time the bull requires it."

Taking down one of his hammers, Sidah told Jomar to hold the head steady on the worktable while he attached the beard to the gilded head with long metal nails that he drove through the backing and into the wooden core. Sidah dropped to his knees in front of the instrument. Instructing Jomar to hold it steady against the lyre's sound box, he attached the bull's head to the lyre with hot tar, then he bound the head to the instrument with long strips of cotton. "The head is heavy with gold and lapis, so these strips must be kept in place until the tar hardens." Sidah floated the cotton shroud over the lyre.

The embellishment of the lyre had been completed, but instead of feeling jubilant, Jomar found all his worries about Zefa crowding him again.

Jomar saw Sidah studying him. "I asked you to put your concerns about Zefa aside, but I see you're too troubled to manage that," Sidah said.

"Even though I know that now she's safe with her little band, she's still in danger," Jomar said. "I've tried to put her out of my mind during the day, but I dream about her at night. I think the high priestess will do something to save you, but I know Malak will come back for Zefa and force her to take the river test."

"If she's innocent, as you think she is, the sacred waters will establish this for all to see."

"I want to believe you, but Zefa can't swim," Jomar said. "She'll fail the test whether or not she took the bead."

"You have no faith in the wisdom of the sacred river?" Sidah asked.

"I'm not certain," Jomar said, aware that Sidah did believe in the test. "It must have happened that innocent people have drowned and guilty ones have been saved. All I'm sure of is that Zefa is innocent *because* she's willing to take the test."

Sidah listened to this outburst without a change of expression. "We see this differently, but—" He broke off as he heard Nari gasp. Then heavy footsteps. Malak swept into the workroom.

"You didn't expect me so soon, did you?" Malak said, his tone smug. "I drove my crew hard, and we finished early. Has the little lyre player decided to come with me or undergo the river test?"

Jomar carefully drew in his breath. "My sister declares her innocence, and will take the test."

Malak looked startled. Clearly he had not expected Zefa's decision, but he quickly took charge of the situation. He turned to Sidah. "Bring the young thief to the bridge over the canal at noon tomorrow. Your wife brought the charge of theft, so she must be present." Malak's lips snapped shut. He left as abruptly as he'd entered.

29 BRIDGE OVER THE CANAL

Sidah shook his head sadly. "Go get Zefa. She must spend the night with us before she faces her ordeal."

"I know you feel the river is a trustworthy judge, but my father made me responsible for my sister," Jomar said. "I can't let her take the test. I'll take it in her place."

Sidah's eyes opened with surprise. "No! Only people accused of a crime can undergo the ordeal."

"I've thought of a way," Jomar said. "Will you tell Malak tomorrow that you and Nari now think I took the bead? He won't believe you, but he'll be forced to let the river decide if I'm guilty or not."

Sidah spoke after a long pause. "I must accept your plan. We'll never know how the river would have judged Zefa, but you'll survive because you didn't take the bead."

Jomar wanted to believe this, but he also was unable to swim.

"Will you bring Zefa to the canal to watch you take the test?" Sidah asked.

Jomar shook his head. "She couldn't bear to look at a stranger's struggle when we first entered the city. She must not see me in the water."

Early the next morning Jomar, Sidah, and Nari left the house. The walk to the canal was like a nightmare from his troubled sleep. The street was crowded with excited people all going toward the canal to witness the ordeal. Halfway to the bridge Sidah put his hand on Jomar's shoulder. Its firm, comforting weight remained there until they finally reached the canal.

Standing on the bridge Jomar looked down at the dirty blue-green water below and felt his knees weaken. The laughter and talk of those already on the bridge was an unwelcome buzz in his ears. Clearly in good spirits, they were waiting as if a celebration were about to begin.

Malak loomed over the crowd, frowning as he looked around. "Where's the girl?" he barked at Sidah.

"She won't be coming," Sidah said. "We thought it best to spare her the agony of seeing her brother take the test."

"Her brother? What are you talking about?" Malak spit out.

"It seems my quick-fingered apprentice tried to blame his sister for something he did himself," Sidah said with feigned anger.

For a moment Malak was at a loss. Then his eyes darted to Nari. "You were the one to accuse the slave girl!"

Nari's chin went up. "My accusation was in error. I couldn't believe this farm boy would repay our kindness by stealing from us."

Malak flung out his hand toward Nari in an angry gesture. Sidah gave her a small, appreciative nod.

Malak spoke to Jomar in a fierce whisper. "I don't care if she took the bead or not, but this scheme could cost you your life." Drawing himself up to his full height, Malak seemed about to lift Jomar up and fling him over the side of the bridge.

Before Malak could act Jomar ducked under his arm and pushed people aside. He opened his mouth wide, sucked in air, then jumped into the water below. Down, down he went into the murky canal. He had planned to spring up from the bottom, but the slippery silt prevented him from securing a firm footing. Thrashing wildly about in the dark water, Jomar lost all sense of direction. He felt his breath slowly leaving his lungs, and he could feel panic entering his mind, his body. Trying to orient himself in the canal, Jomar turned endlessly in the water.

A weak light broke through above him! Suddenly remembering his panicked thrashing in the water when his reed boat sank, Jomar began to slowly and deliberately move his arms in wide circles. Amazingly he rose up! Now he began moving his legs in the same circular movement, and found this doubled the speed of his rise to the surface. His head came out of the water and into the sunlight just before he thought his aching lungs would burst! Jomar spat out water, gulped in air, but never stopped moving his arms and legs. With his ears cleared he heard shouts and snatches of heated conversation:

"Innocent! I told you he'd come up!"

"But he was under for a long time!"

"The banks are steep . . . hard for him to climb out of the canal!"

Without the buoyancy of the deep water, Jomar's limbs now seemed to be made of stone. He could breathe, but he made no progress as he tried to move toward the bank. Suddenly he saw a blur of someone rushing toward the water from the bank high above him. Gamil!

Holding his ball high above his head, Gamil jumped feetfirst into the water. He disappeared for an instant, then surfaced. "Hang on to it!" he yelled, then threw his ball toward Jomar before going under yet again.

Jomar reached up and grabbed the inflated bladder. By clasping it to his chest with both hands, he kept his upper body out of the water, and used his waning strength to move his legs. But instead of moving toward the bank, he spun in a circle. While he turned he saw Gamil flailing his arms and sputtering each time his head rose from the canal. Jomar used one arm to grasp the ball and the other to paddle himself toward Gamil. Jomar felt the bank under his feet as soon as he reached him. Letting go of the ball, he held Gamil's head above the water. Clutching at the reeds that grew along the slope, he slowly pulled himself and Gamil out of the canal.

As they made their way up the incline, Jomar lost his grip on the smooth, slippery plants and started to slide back toward the cloudy water. Gamil grabbed his wrists to stop the fall, then together they slowly climbed up the steep bank. When they reached the top, they sprawled flat on their stomachs gasping for breath. Finally they stood with their hands on their knees, their heads down. When their breathing grew steady, they looked up at each other. Grinning with relief, they moved forward and pounded each other on the back.

On the bridge Malak was moving toward them with Sidah and Nari close behind. "You've tricked me, you've all tricked me!" Malak shouted. "The wrong person was in the water! The little slave girl is the guilty one!" He rushed at Jomar, one arm raised to strike him.

Sidah moved in and grabbed his arm. "The test has proved the boy innocent," he shouted, and the crowd roared its approval.

Standing close to Malak, Jomar spoke in a manly tone he didn't know he possessed. "You'd be wise to leave both Sidah and my sister alone. The high priestess Bittatti has already punished you once. Now she's angry that you've put the temple's master goldsmith in jeopardy."

Malak stopped, his face contorted with fear. "The high priestess? She knows of this?" He opened his mouth to say something more, but no words came out. He wheeled around, almost colliding with Sidah and Nari in his rush to leave. As he hurried away, Malak's towering figure slowly diminished in size until it disappeared.

30 A SILENCE BROKEN

With Nari close behind him, Sidah threw his arms around Jomar and hugged him close. "Your innocence saved you. I told you the river is wise!" Then he spoke in a whispery voice full of tears. "I never would have recovered if the waters had taken both you and Abban."

Jomar returned the embrace. "Thank you for letting me take the test in Zefa's place." He turned to Gamil. "I'm standing here because of you. When I was tiring, your ball kept me afloat. When I slipped on the bank, you pulled me up."

Gamil smiled. "We saved each other."

"We did, but why risk your life to save mine?"

"I saw you all leave the house early," Gamil said in a guarded voice. "I heard people on the street talking about an ordeal to be held on the bridge. . . ." He faltered. "An ordeal that—that had to do with the theft of a bead."

Sidah's eyes were hard with suspicion. "What do you know about this?"

Gamil looked at the ground instead of answering.

"You must tell us!" Jomar said.

"I've tried to tell you over and over again," Gamil said, "but you were always in a hurry, too busy to listen to me."

"I'll listen to you now," Jomar said with a clutch of guilt.

"Before you do, I want to stop at my house," Gamil said, his face tense. They walked to Gamil's home in an uneasy silence, then waited for him to come out. When he did he came up to Sidah and slowly opened his clenched fist. "I'm the one who should have taken the river test."

On his open palm lay the missing lapis bead.

Nari gasped. "How did you get that bead?"

"You stole it!" Sidah thundered. With a swipe of his hand, he took the bead from Gamil's palm.

Gamil locked his eyes on Sidah. "No! That day,

the day of Abban's death, he stopped to show me this bead on his way to the harbor. He was so proud of his work on Bittatti's necklace, especially the holes he drilled in the lapis beads. He was in a hurry to go the harbor to inspect some gems. He told me I should keep the bead until he returned, thinking it would be safer at my house than on the waterfront. Abban rushed off." Gamil blinked back tears. "He never came back."

"But you kept it!" Sidah said. "Why didn't you return it long ago?"

Now tears fell down Gamil's cheeks. "I didn't want you to know that Abban disobeyed you by taking the bead out of the workshop." He struggled to continue. "I wanted you to have only good memories of your son."

Gamil's words rang true to Jomar, and he could sense Sidah's anger evaporating like morning mist on the marsh lake.

Sidah looked hard at Gamil, then sighed. "You've been a good friend to my son, even after his death. Come to the house this afternoon for Abban's funeral ceremony. We must hold it today because soon they'll come to take away the temple lyre we've been working on."

Nari put a hand on Gamil's arm. "Jomar's sister will play on the lyre and sing a praise song for our son—for your friend."

Gamil nodded his acceptance to the invitation and returned to his house. Nari hurried ahead to prepare for the ceremony.

Sidah spoke in a somber tone when he and Jomar were alone. "How could I have been so sure that Zefa took the bead? I had no evidence, no proof."

Jomar spoke with effort. "You'd known her for only a day when the bead was found missing. I've known her all her life and I believed her guilty." His voice broke. "And she's my sister."

Sidah patted Jomar's shoulder. "Go to the bazaar and bring back Zefa."

31 GIFTS

Jomar hurried through the winding streets to the bazaar. This time the music of the little band drew him like a lodestone. When he joined the people listening to the music, Zefa nodded to him as they played. She was singing her song to the sungod, repeating the last line before the song came to an end: *"Bold Utu battles darkness to defeat the night."* Jomar went up to her. "Your song is fine, Zefa. The group is stronger because of you."

Zefa was as thin and dirty as before, but her smile lit up her face. "This is the first time you've had anything good to say about my music."

Jomar was stung by the truth of what she said, but her smile helped him to continue. "The lyre is finished, so Abban's funeral must be held today before it's taken to the temple. Let's start off—I have important things to tell you on the way."

But Zefa didn't move. "I've composed a song for Abban, but I'm frightened that Malak will see me."

"We need to cover your hair so you'll look like a boy," Jomar said.

A member of the band stepped forward holding out her scarf. Zefa wrapped it carefully around her head so that her long hair was tucked inside. Jomar watched with envy at the affection shown as she said goodbye to her friends.

As soon as they started the walk to Sidah's house, Jomar exploded with his news. "The bead's been found! You're innocent—just as you've said you were."

"My own words didn't convince you," Zefa said coolly, "so now there's proof that I'm not a thief."

Jomar put his arm around her. "I've wronged you, Zefa. Your denial should have been more than enough."

Her face softened as she stared at him. "Tell me how the bead was discovered."

While Jomar told her the linked stories of the missing lapis bead and the river ordeal, Zefa's eyes grew large with wonder. When he stopped speaking she spoke in a voice full of emotion. "I know you don't believe in the wisdom of the river, so taking the test in my place took courage."

"Zefa, don't go back to the bazaar," Jomar pleaded. "I'll find a way to keep you safe at Sidah's house."

"You heard Nari tell me that I'd have to leave on the day the lyre was finished," Zefa said. Then she looked thoughtful instead of angry. "Living with Nari was hard, but I think I know why she's been so mean to us."

"How can you know this?" Jomar asked.

"I know because I know," Zefa said, glancing at him with irritation. "Do you remember my favorite pig, the one I'd taken care of since the moment he was born? He disappeared one day, and I found him dead in a deep irrigation ditch." She looked up at Jomar. "I didn't want to be around pigs for a long, long time because I'd lost the one I loved the most."

"I remember," Jomar said. "You made up a praise song for him."

"And you made fun of me."

Jomar could feel his cheeks redden. He hadn't realized how deeply felt his sister's song had been. "I think you're right, Zefa. When Nari looks at us, living in her house, she can only think of Abban who should be there instead of us." They walked on together in silence.

When they entered Sidah's house, Nari went up to Zefa as if to envelop her in her arms, then stopped. "I now know you didn't take the bead. Even when I thought you did, I never should have told Malak. You lived under my roof and needed my sheltering, and I failed to protect you." Nari now spoke in a voice filled with tears. "You've answered my cruelty with kindness, Zefa, and I plead for your forgiveness."

Zefa gazed at Nari, hesitated, then embraced her. As Sidah and Jomar watched, Nari slowly put her arms around Zefa.

Zefa pointed to her worn tunic. "I must wash myself before the ceremony."

"Wait. I've something to give you." Nari slid out a flat reed basket from underneath her cot. Opening it, she held up a long, ivory-colored tunic of finely woven linen. "I wore this at my wedding, and was saving it for Abban's wife. I give it to you, Zefa, and I'd be pleased if you wore it for the ceremony."

Zefa smiled and cradled Nari's gift in her arms as she walked to the washroom. When she returned she was transformed. She had circled her braided hair twice around her head, and Nari's close-fitting gown, which left one shoulder bare, fit perfectly.

A soft knock. Sidah greeted Gamil at the door. After Jomar introduced him to Zefa, he gazed at her with admiration, but seemed too shy to speak. They sat at the table for the little feast of wheat porridge covered with sweet date syrup that Nari had prepared to mark the ceremony.

"We've had a frightening morning that ended well," Sidah said. He opened his hand to reveal the lapis bead on his outstretched palm. "Zefa, I wish I could give you this bead that has brought you only grief, but it belongs to the temple."

Zefa took up the small blue gem flecked with yellow and studied it closely. "It still looks like it fell from the starry night sky." She returned it to Sidah. "You're kind to wish it were mine."

"Abban made this bead out of a bit of lapis," Jomar said. "Could it be a part of the ceremony in some way?"

Sidah looked surprised, then pleased. "A good thought, Jomar. The bead will represent Abban today." Holding it in one fisted hand, Sidah beckoned the others to follow him into the workshop.

Nari had already pushed the tables and equipment against the walls, and now the lyre stood alone in the center of the room. Jomar heard Zefa gasp when she saw the bull's head. And he saw for the first time that the lyre resembled the body of a bull, and the size and position of the head were exactly right. The long, soaring horns, vivid eyes, and beard of dark blue lapis were in perfect harmony with each other. Like a deity the bull seemed to stand apart from them and from all the difficulties that had accompanied its creation.

Zefa walked to the lyre and stood there quietly, one hand resting against the silent strings. Moments passed. Jomar grew uneasy until he realized what Zefa was doing. The substitution of the bead for Abban's body had changed the meaning of the ceremony, so his sister was changing the words to the song as she stood there. Finally Zefa raised her hands to the strings, but then footsteps were heard instead of music.

Kurgal, the music director, entered the workshop, trailed by two husky guards. The three men stopped short when they saw the lyre.

"Sidah, this is superb work, more glorious than anything I'd even hoped for!" Kurgal said.

"Your words are welcome," Sidah said. "Before you remove the lyre, will you allow this young girl to sing a praise song in honor of my son?"

Kurgal's eyebrows shot up. "This child is to play on the temple lyre?"

Zefa looked to Sidah for guidance.

Sidah silently mouthed one word. "Begin."

32 SONG FOR ABBAN

Despite the tension in the room, Jomar felt calm when Zefa's fingers began to strum the lyre. With his eyes closed, he heard the flowing music as Zefa's pure voice joined the deep sounds of the lyre:

"We sing now of Abban,
Whose hands were strong and skillful,
Who departed from this dwelling
Leaving empty places in the heart.

We sing now of Abban,
Whose spirit seeks a dwelling
Amid work he joyfully created
With gold and hammer, lapis and tong.

We sing now of Abban,
Who once more dwells among us,

Whose parents' hearts are lifted—
His restless spirit has come home."

Jomar knew the end of the song was near when Zefa began to repeat the last line of the last verse. But this time, with a subtle shift of rhythm, her voice and the strumming of the lyre expressed a mood less melancholy and more accepting. Jomar opened his eyes and looked at Sidah and Nari. From their rapt faces, he knew that Zefa's music had fallen like rain upon an arid field.

Too full of feeling to speak, Gamil started to leave the house, but Nari held him back with a hand on his arm. "Zefa's song brings peace to Abban and to us all. I'm coming with you to visit your mother. I'll see her every day, as I used to do, so you can go back to your job."

Gamil smiled at her with teary eyes. "We'll welcome this." He and Nari left the house together.

Kurgal spoke to Sidah. "I had no intention of interrupting so solemn an occasion. The high priestess ordered me to come to your house to listen to a young girl play and sing. I thought I could do so at the same time I removed the lyre from your work-shop." He frowned. "I did not think the girl would be playing on this lyre."

Sidah nodded to indicate he had heard the direc-tor, but said nothing.

Kurgal waited a moment, then turned to Zefa. "It's clear you're without training, but you played well, and your song was full of feeling. I'm selecting you to be a member of the temple musicians. Like the others you'll be housed, clothed, and fed at the temple. Someday you may be asked to play on this lyre again, but only after a long period of study."

"Thank you," Zefa whispered, "but do you know about Malak . . . and me?"

"I do," Kurgal said. "You and Sidah have no rea-son to fear him, because the high priestess has used her powers well. She has decreed that Malak is no longer a temple official, and you are no longer a slave."

Jomar rejoiced at Bittatti's intervention, but thought with a pang of the loss of Zefa from his life. "Will I ever be able to see my sister?" he asked the music director.

Kurgal nodded. "The temple will not be her

prison. Her training will be rigorous, but she can come here when she has time to do so." He turned to Zefa. "Gather your things together. We'll go to the new dwelling place of both you and the lyre."

Zefa's face was one of slow comprehension of what was happening to her. "I will have a life of music," she said softly.

Kurgal gave a slight smile, then looked around the workshop. "Do you have any unused gold for me to take back to the treasury?"

Jomar pointed to the small fragment of gold that he'd seen clinging to the edge of the flat stone.

"Your apprentice is honest," the director said to Sidah. "Keep the gold as a gift of gratitude from the temple."

"Here's something else that belongs to the temple," Sidah said, holding out the lapis bead. "For the ceremony today, this precious gem contained the spirit of my precious—" he hesitated, "—our precious son."

Kurgal held up his palm. "Keep the bead as well, so Abban's spirit will always stay with you in your dwelling."

Sidah bent his head low in appreciation. For the

last time he billowed out the cotton cover, which settled gracefully over the lyre. Kurgal gave a signal to the guards, who carefully shouldered the great instrument and walked slowly out of the workroom.

After Jomar had lifted Zefa's basket to her shoulders, she turned and spoke to him. "All this happened because you made me a lyre so long ago."

"I made you a toy, Zefa," Jomar said. "You took the toy and made music with it—music that moves people who know how to listen."

Zefa's face filled with radiance, and she threw her arms around him. "Now you're more than my brother. You're my friend." Jomar embraced her and watched as Zefa bowed to Sidah and Nari and left the house with the music director. Her new life was beginning—and so was his.

33 THE RIVER IS RISING

Sidah brought the worktables out from the walls.

"The ceremony was so important, Jomar. Because of you and Zefa, our son had a proper funeral, and Nari's heart has softened."

"You told me that she used to laugh a lot," Jomar said. "Perhaps she will again."

Sidah sighed. "I would welcome this. Now that the lyre is finished, what have you decided about staying here or returning home?"

Instead of answering, Jomar joined Sidah in rearranging the room.

Sidah waited. "You're quiet. You're not sure?"

In that instant Jomar knew he was sure. "It's so hard to know that I can't see my parents again, but I want to stay with you and work to become a goldsmith—a fine one, like you."

"I'm glad you're staying with me. But you've misunderstood the rules that govern apprentices and their masters," Sidah said. "You can't live with your parents, but you can still see them. Word could be sent to the farm that they should come to the city for the great new year ceremony. Zefa will be a part of the celebration, and they'll be able to see the lyre you helped create."

"I can see them again!" Jomar said. "But how will they know to come here?"

"Perhaps the slave Qat-nu could go to the farm and invite them," Sidah said.

Jomar nodded. "Zefa hoped the gods would reward Qat-nu for his kindness to us. He'll no longer be working under Malak, and my father will need help in bringing the fields back to life. Do you think he could take my place on the farm? My parents are good and kind people, and this could be Qat-nu's reward."

"I'll speak to an official at the temple to see if this can be arranged." Sidah bent to recover the bit of gold. "I was aware of this fragment and glad you called attention to it. There's just enough gold to make a small bead for Zefa."

"You told me how difficult it is to make these little beads," Jomar said. "Now I'll be able to watch you do it."

"Tomorrow we'll do it together," Sidah said. "My hope is this gift will heal all wounds."

Sidah looked around the empty workshop. "This has been a long and demanding day. I need to relax with my friends." He turned to leave the house. "Do what you like—just be home in time for the evening meal."

Nari had cleaned the workroom for the ceremony, so there was no need for him to sweep or return the tools to their hooks. The daily task of making order out of disorder was strangely satisfying, but now the afternoon stretched ahead of him, empty.

Jomar sat at one of the worktables and cradled his head on his arms. He thought of the long morning filled with terror and reconciliation. He would stay with the goldsmith, but he knew he would miss working alongside his father to restore the farm to growth and abundance. In the quiet workshop he imagined hearing squawking birds flying low over freshly seeded fields. He could see in his mind the new, bright green shoots of date palms.

He raised his head and moved his hands as if touching the smooth, wet skin of the little calf born in hard times. Jomar thought of the golden bull lyre that had also experienced a difficult birth into the world. He could not leave this place where such beauty was created.

Currents of energy flooded Jomar's body. He sprang up and ran outside. "Gamil," he called out. "Sidah heard that the snows in the northern mountains are finally melting! Let's go to the river and see if the water has started to rise."

AUTHOR'S NOTE

Many years ago, in an auditorium filled with rapt listeners, I listened to a lullaby played on a reproduction of a 4,750-year-old Mesopotamian lyre. The experience has stayed with me, connecting me to the people who soothed their babies long ago with that haunting melody. *The Golden Bull* grew out of this memory.

Jomar and Zefa, creatures of my imagination, dwelt in southern Mesopotamia, now Iraq, in 2600 BC. How is it possible to accurately portray how they lived on their farm and in the once-vibrant city of Ur? One significant source of information has been the accumulation and decoding of thousands of clay tablets covered with a wedge-shaped script called *cuneiform*. This remarkable invention, thought to be the first written language in history, was originally designed to record everyday concerns when human memory could no longer accurately store this information. Trained scribes recorded business transactions, the inventories of storage granaries, and the payments of fines and taxes. Gradually, the scope of subject matter expanded to include legends and poems, lists of kings and their triumphant battles, musical notation, astronomical observations—anything and everything that these creative people wanted to remember.

Our understanding of how the people of Mesopotamia lived is also based on the work of archaeologists whose efforts have revealed complex irrigation systems, elaborate temple ruins, and the living quarters of common people. In the 1920s a joint expedition by the British Museum and the University of Pennsylvania was mounted to excavate the buried ruins of Ur. British archaeologist C. Leonard Woolley and his team unearthed a most astonishing discovery: a cemetery of sixteen undisturbed tombs filled with human remains and grave goods made by highly skilled craftsmen—such as the goldsmith Sidah in this book.

Woolley called this burial site the Royal Tombs

of Ur, although it has never been determined if those buried were royalty or temple officials. Among the treasures found were intricate wreaths and jewelry, a gold drinking straw over four feet long, skillfully carved cylinder seals, and the magnificent golden bull lyre. All are important elements in my story. Today these stunning burial goods may be seen in the University of Pennsylvania Museum of Archaeology and Anthropology, the British Museum, and the National Museum of Iraq in Baghdad.

The city of Ur, located on the western bank of the Euphrates River, is now largely covered with sand. In ancient times the annual flooding of the river had been tamed by an ingenious irrigation system of canals, dikes, and reservoirs that enabled fields and gardens to flourish. This formerly productive region is referred to today as the Fertile Crescent. Jomar and his family, however, experienced a severe drought, which sets the story in motion. As Jomar and Zefa find out, the Euphrates was so crucial to the life of the area that it was believed the river could determine the guilt or innocence of a person accused of wrongdoing.

The farmlands surrounding Ur were largely owned by the great temple of the moongod, and the maintenance of the irrigation system was supervised by temple officials. A proportion of the produce and livestock of the farms was demanded as tribute to the temple in order to maintain its staff of administrators, scribes, musicians, and craftsmen.

Because the region was devoid of important natural resources, the temple also used this tribute as barter for metals, stone, timber, and gems. These highly desirable commodities were secured by trade with the area that is now Egypt, Afghanistan, Iran, India, and Pakistan. Ur could not have survived for three thousand years without these far-reaching exchanges.

Slavery was an integral part of Mesopotamian society. Soldiers defeated in battle with neighboring cities were taken into slavery, as were people convicted of crimes or those unable to pay their debts. Children could be enslaved if found without a parent far from home, as Zefa was, or they could be sold into slavery by their parents. But slaves could be freed by a powerful authority, such as the high priestess in the story.

In the Mesopotamian belief system, humans had been created only to support and maintain the governing gods. Great attention was paid to the cycles of the sun and moon, birth and death, planting and reaping, and the ebb and flow of their mighty rivers. These concerns were embodied by a pantheon of gods and goddesses who demanded homage and gifts to prevent them from turning against their worshipers.

There were also many minor deities, such as Ninkasi, the goddess of beer, for whom Zefa creates a song. Each city-state had its own patron deity, such as the moongod Nanna, who was thought to inhabit the great temple of Ur. In ceremonies such as the celebration of the new year, bounty from farmers and merchants was displayed, sheep and cattle were sacrificed, and elaborate performances were presented by temple dancers and musicians.

Music was an important element in almost every aspect of life in ancient Mesopotamia, and artwork frequently depicts people playing various instruments. The kinds of songs Zefa sings are known to us through cuneiform tablets that have preserved religious hymns, love songs, praise songs, and lullabies. The lives of Jomar and Zefa were different from our own in many ways, but the songs remind us of our deep and enduring similarities.

ACKNOWLEDGMENTS

The following scholars have generously given me their time, expertise, and life-giving encouragement:

Virginia Greene, senior conservator, University of Pennsylvania Museum of Archaeology and Anthropology, Philadelphia, PA

Anne D. Kilmer, PhD, professor of the Department of Near Eastern Studies, University of California, Berkeley, CA

Pieter Meyers, PhD, senior research conservation chemist, Los Angeles County Museum of Art, Los Angeles, CA

Denise Schmandt-Besserat, PhD, professor of Art and Middle Eastern Studies, University of Texas at Austin, TX